ABOARD BLACKBEARD'S QUEEN

To: Rose

Hope you enjoy
this adventure!
Arrr!
Robin Reams

ABOARD BLACKBEARD'S QUEEN

Robin Reams

Published by
Wisdom House Books Inc.

ABOARD BLACKBEARD'S QUEEN

Published by Wisdom House Books, Inc.
Chapel Hill, North Carolina 27517 USA
www.wisdomhousebooks.com

Wisdom House Books is committed to excellence in the publishing industry.

Cover and Interior Design by Ted Ruybal
Cover photography by Robin Reams

Published in the United States of America

Paperback ISBN: 979-8-9871896-0-3
Library of Congress Control Number: 2023901888

1. YAF001010 | YOUNG ADULT FICTION / Action & Adventure / Pirates
2. YAF002040 | YOUNG ADULT FICTION / Animals / Pets
3. YAF024000 | YOUNG ADULT FICTION / Historical / General

First Edition

25 24 23 22 21 20 / 10 9 8 7 6 5 4 3 2 1

Dedicated to my co-authors: God and my Savior, Jesus Christ.
Also, in loving memory of my sister.
Holly Reams 1993–2009

I couldn't have written this without constant
help from Heaven. I love you so much!

"Be strong and of good courage; do not be afraid,
nor be dismayed, for the LORD your God is with you
wherever you go."

~JOSHUA 1:9

Trust in the LORD with all your heart,
And lean not on your own understanding; In all your ways
acknowledge Him, And He shall direct your paths.

~PROVERBS 3:5-6

Contents

Acknowledgments

Thank you, God, for Your unfailing love and constant guidance. The ability to write stories is a gift that I am honored to have. To my family, friends, and readers, I extend my heartfelt thanks for your support and prayers. Of course, to my sister, Holly, who enjoyed history as much as I do and has left me with so many memories, including the hours spent researching family history. Our shared interest in Blackbeard and visiting historical sites during our childhood ignited my imagination while working on this book. Thanks, Mom and Dad, for helping me continue to pursue my love of writing.

Author's Note

As much as possible I used real facts and events as a foundation for this story, but my own imagination created this book. This adventure is historical fiction. It takes a lot of hard work to gather the necessary information to make historical fiction realistic. I have studied books on piracy, navigation, sailing ships, native plants and animals, colonial living, and layouts of islands and towns. Additionally, I spent many hours researching colonial documents, attending pirate reenactments, visiting museums, walking historical sites, and talking to historians. Although the main character is my creation, many of the supporting characters are based on real people I discovered by digging into the available records. I took artistic liberties with their personalities and features since they are fictional characters in my story. For the most part, the places mentioned in this book are real locations, and I tried to describe them as close to what they were in 1718. Historical researchers learn new things about the past every day, so it will be interesting to see what they uncover in the future.

Get Ready Mate ~ It's Time To Set Sail . . .

CHAPTER ONE

Bad Omen

Steady gusts of wind blew through Cooper's orange fur as he stood on a crate looking at the ocean. Even with his claws out he had to be careful not to lose his balance. Falling over the railing and into the water would be a terrible fate.

Being a pirate cat was difficult enough without the dangers of ship life. Cooper knew the pirates wouldn't save him if he fell overboard. Then again, he doubted the captain from his previous sailing mission would have either.

"Land ho!" shouted a voice from the top of the ship's rigging.

Cooper looked up into the ropes and sails. His green eyes spotted a man holding onto the main mast with a spyglass in his hand. The man told the gathered pirate crew down below that he spotted an island ahead.

Cheers erupted from the crew as Cooper shivered at the news. Part of him was glad the ship would be returning to the island, but he also knew the other pirates anchored there were going to be very mad. To make matters worse, the leader of the pirates on the island was Captain Blackbeard, a man everyone feared.

"Tell Captain Bonnet land is in sight," one of the pirates ordered.

"Don't bother with him. Just get the sails turned," another replied.

Their attitude toward the ship's captain didn't surprise Cooper. He figured it was only a matter of time before the crew pushed the captain aside, especially after he almost got them killed. Captain Stede Bonnet was far from a qualified leader, which was why the pirates were heading back to the island to rejoin Blackbeard's crew.

Thankfully, Cooper's dealing with the pirates hadn't been as bad as he originally feared, though he tried to stay out of their way. It had been five moons since Blackbeard's pirates captured the ship Cooper sailed on. Before then, Cooper was just a normal ship's cat with the simple but important duty to keep the mouse population low.

This journey had been Cooper's first assignment and from the start it was nothing but trouble. One bad thing after another seemed to happen to the great ship, which the French had named *La Concorde*.

The French ship had left France with a cargo of fabric and a new mouser. Right away, Cooper discovered being a mouser was hard. The bad weather didn't help things. By the time the ship made it to Africa, Cooper was ready to quit. He had hoped the ship's captain would quickly sell the fabric and head back to France, but that didn't happen.

Instead, the captain traded the boatload of fabric for five hundred and sixteen captive Africans and twenty pounds of gold dust. With a full load of captives, the *La Concorde* set sail for the islands of the Caribbean.

Travel was slow with all the added weight. Before long they met a fleet of ships coming toward them. By the time the captain realized they were pirates it was too late. The *La Concorde* had so many people onboard they couldn't outrun them.

In no time, the pirates had taken over the ship. Cooper overheard the sailors say that this group of pirates were under the leadership of the feared captain, Blackbeard. After hearing the stories of how mean Blackbeard was, Cooper was so scared he didn't know what to do. He tried to hide, but the pirates found him anyway.

To his surprise, Blackbeard wanted to keep Cooper as another mouser. They kept the gold and some of the captives, too. The pirates also decided they wanted to add the *La Concorde* to their fleet of ships. Blackbeard ordered his men to dump all the remaining captives and sailors on a deserted island. Then the fleet sailed away with their prize ship *La Concorde* leading the way.

Even after all this time, Cooper still had nightmares of the capture. His nervousness around the pirates only added to his other problem of not being able to fulfill his mouser duties. It wasn't the mice he had an issue with. He was fearful of the giant rats.

"Arrrr! Get out of the way!" a pirate shouted as he waved his arms at Cooper to scare him.

Cooper instinctively folded his ears back as he jumped off the crate and scurried to the back of the ship. Once he was safely out of the way, he watched the crew move the sails until the wind caught the stiff cloth.

"What are you doing, Coop?" asked a squeaky voice above him.

Knowing the voice belonged to his new friend, Cooper looked up at the ropes crisscrossed over his head. Sure enough, Como, the spider monkey, was hanging upside down from the ropes by his long tail. The little brown monkey loved playing in the ship's rigging and causing mischief.

"I was looking at the ocean, but one of the pirates got mad. He probably thought I was going to cause trouble again," Cooper said.

"Trouble? That's not you, Coop. If anyone is trouble, it's me!" Como laughed as he did a flip and landed on the wooden deck.

Cooper smiled at his little friend. Como was the only one who had ever called him Coop, but he didn't care. It was good to have a friend, even if he did seem to get into a lot of trouble.

In the short time Cooper had been on the ship, he had learned a lot from Como. The little spider monkey had explained that the pirates called this ship the *Revenge.* It was under the direction of Captain Stede Bonnet, although all the ships in the fleet had to obey the main pirate, Captain Blackbeard.

From what Cooper understood, Como had been on the *Revenge* for nearly a year. The pirates captured him from his home island and decided to keep him because Captain Bonnet thought Como was entertaining.

"Do you think Captain Blackbeard will be mad when we get back to the island?" Cooper asked, remembering the stories Como had told him.

"I'm sure things will be tense. Captain Stede really messed up this time. He thought he could handle leading his own mission, but I guess he wasn't ready. Blackbeard won't be too happy to hear that these pirates couldn't capture the ship," Como replied.

Cooper thought about the ship Como was referring to. The *Protestant Caesar* was supposed to be an easy target, but Stede Bonnet's poor decisions forced the pirates to abandon their prize ship. To make matters worse, they almost got themselves captured.

By now the crew was busily moving around the deck trying to keep the ship on course. Captain Stede Bonnet came out of his cabin at the back of the boat to see their progress. He wore a long, light gray coat and a three-cornered hat with a bright red feather in it. In Cooper's opinion, Bonnet acted too silly to be a feared pirate.

Bonnet shouted at several members of his crew, but they seemed to be ignoring him. Although their disobedience appeared to upset Bonnet, he didn't make any threats to them. Instead, he just walked around the deck watching the men do their work while they gave him looks of disgust.

Before long, the *Revenge* arrived at Turneffe Island. Como scampered up the ropes to get a better look while Cooper jumped up on a stool in the back corner of the deck so he could see over the railing.

The tropical island rose out of the ocean off the coast of Belize. From Cooper's perch, he watched and waited as the pirates sailed around the point of the island and into the lagoon. His heart beat faster in his chest as his green eyes spotted the *La Concorde* anchored inside. About half of Blackbeard's crew were on the beach.

As soon as the *Revenge* entered the lagoon, they fired off four empty cannon shots to announce their arrival. Cooper remembered Como telling him that four shots were a signal that they were friends of the other ship. It was a rule to keep from spooking other pirate ships to avoid an attack.

Members of Blackbeard's crew still on the *La Concorde* returned the signal by firing their guns. Knowing it was safe to enter, the crew of the *Revenge* sailed the ship further into the lagoon and anchored it beside the *La Concorde*. Then they prepared to lower the small boat in the center of the deck into the water so they could row ashore.

"We have arrived!" Como shouted excitedly as he swung from one rope to another down to where Cooper waited.

"You sound excited. Aren't you scared of what might happen between Captain Bonnet and Captain Blackbeard?" Cooper asked.

"Why should we be scared? You're a ship's cat and I'm a funny little spider monkey. Just look at that island. It's a new adventure, Coop!"

Cooper looked at the palm trees dotting the sandy beach. Como was right. Why should he be worried?

"Alright, Captain," one of the pirates said to Bonnet. "We're anchored and ready to go ashore."

"Great! Let's get the periauger in the water then," Bonnet replied.

The gathered crew looked at each other. They obviously had something on their minds. Finally, one of them stepped forward.

"Captain, don't ye need to be on the first trip ashore?"

"It really doesn't matter," Bonnet answered.

"As the leader of our ship, we think ye should. Why don't ye take them with ye?" the pirate added as he pointed at Cooper and Como.

Fear gripped Cooper's heart as he glanced at Como. Even the little monkey looked a bit uneasy.

"What for?" Bonnet wanted to know.

"I'll tell ye what for!" another pirate exploded. He forced his way to the front of the group and shoved a stubby finger in Cooper's face. "This whole mission failed because of that thing."

Cooper folded his ears and squatted as close to the deck as possible. Como tried to stand up for him, but of course the pirates couldn't understand what he was saying. All they heard were barks and squeals, which prompted another crewmate to jump into the conversation.

"Ye might as well take that monkey with ye, too. He's a nuisance! Half the time he's in our way when we're working with the sails, and he likes to steal things."

"He's just playing," Bonnet interrupted. "As for Cooper, we need a ship's cat."

"That is no ship's cat. No wonder all the other ships we have had in the fleet didn't want him. I thought it was odd these past few months when they kept passing him around. He's a bad omen," the pirate continued.

"What makes ye think Cooper has brought us bad luck?" Bonnet asked.

"He's orange! Every true pirate knows that black cats bring a ship good luck. Things have been going bad for us ever since ye agreed to take him. I would have thrown him overboard myself, but that would have made our luck worse."

"I won't let ye hurt him," Bonnet insisted. "I like creatures with character and his orange fur only proves he is special and destined for greatness."

The pirate snorted. "Ye don't have to worry about me laying a hand on that cat. The legend is clear. If a cat goes overboard on purpose or by accident the bad omen never leaves the ship. Nay, it's best for ye to take him ashore."

Stede Bonnet didn't argue with the crew. Instead, he went to his cabin. Moments later he returned with a wooden cage. He set it down in front of Cooper and Como, who immediately started to climb the ropes to escape. Not being able to follow his friend,

Cooper had no choice but to get himself trapped.

Hissing in protest, Cooper put up a fight, but honestly, he was glad. After hearing how the pirates felt about him, he really didn't want to stay onboard the *Revenge*. There was no telling what they would do to him.

As Stede Bonnet lowered him into the wooden cage, Cooper looked up into the sails and rigging trying to spot his friend. He longed to have Como's company on this new adventure. Eventually he spotted Como hanging by his tail near the top of the mast. The pirates weren't happy about him being up there, but they obviously weren't going to wait for him to come down.

The pirate crew hastily put Cooper's cage into the periauger and quickly hoisted it over the edge of the ship's railing. In no time, they had the small periauger boat in the water and had thrown down the rope ladder so their captain could climb down.

"Como! Como!" Cooper yelled, hoping his friend could hear him.

The periauger rocked back and forth on the water as Captain Bonnet and four members of his crew climbed down the ladder and sat on the boards. Two of them grabbed the oars and pushed off from the ship as something fell from the *Revenge*'s railing and landed on top of Cooper's cage.

To Cooper's relief, it was Como! The little monkey didn't seem injured from the fall. He smiled as Captain Bonnet scooped him up and put him in the cage with Cooper.

"I didn't think I was ever going to see you again," Cooper said.

"Well, I wasn't going to let them catch me, but I didn't want to lose my new friend. Besides, I couldn't let you go on an adventure without me," Como replied.

Cooper grinned. "Everyone knows adventures are more fun when you have someone to share them with. I'm so glad you came!"

The two friends settled down beside each other for the remainder of the journey to the island. Soon, they were near enough for the four pirates to get out of the periauger and drag the boat up on land while Captain Bonnet waited with Cooper and Como.

As the pirates hoisted them out of the periauger, Cooper got his first up close look at Turneffe Island. He was just beginning to get excited when someone walked up. The man was tall and dressed in black, but it was his thick black beard that gave away his identity. This was the famed pirate, Captain Blackbeard.

"I wasn't expecting to see ye so soon," Blackbeard said as he reached to shake Stede Bonnet's hand.

"We ran into a little situation," Bonnet replied.

"What do ye mean?"

Bonnet nervously rubbed his chin. He then began to tell Blackbeard the story of how his crew had spotted and tracked down the prize ship. By the time Bonnet told the part about the prize ship attacking them and almost sinking the *Revenge*, Blackbeard was shaking his head.

"Ye mean to say they not only got away, but also nearly killed ye?" Blackbeard asked.

"I don't think they could have killed us," Bonnet replied.

"If we had been any closer their cannon shots may have sunk our ship," one of Bonnet's crew interrupted. "We can't keep going on like this. Do ye have any advice, Captain Blackbeard?"

"Go tell the rest of ye crew to come ashore so we can talk this over," Blackbeard ordered.

"What is there to talk about?" Bonnet wanted to know.

Two of the four pirates ignored their captain as they followed Blackbeard's orders. They climbed back into the periauger boat and started rowing back to the *Revenge*. Meanwhile, Blackbeard offered Stede a drink of brandy and encouraged him to rest under the shade of a nearby palm tree.

"The turtle soup is ready to eat, Captain," an older pirate told Blackbeard.

The barefooted man was standing near a cook pit stirring the contents of a large pot. He wore striped pants and a faded blue shirt.

"Good. Tell the men they won't get seconds tonight, Cookie. We weren't planning on this many mouths to feed," Blackbeard replied.

When the rest of the pirates arrived on the island, they joined Blackbeard's crew, who were already eating. Even Cooper and Como got a bowl of the turtle soup to share.

Cooper licked his whiskers as he enjoyed the tasty soup. Como, who liked to eat fruit and nuts, wasn't as interested in it, but he didn't complain. There was no telling when they might get another meal.

After most of the pirates had finished eating, Captain Blackbeard called the men together. He suggested that the crew of the *Revenge* hold a vote. Wondering what this meant, Cooper sat up straight so he could hear better.

To his surprise, the pirates all voted to demote Captain Stede Bonnet and to have someone else be their captain. Stede was so shocked by this news he nearly fainted.

"What about me?" he protested. "Where am I supposed to go?"

"Ye can join me as co-captain of *Queen Anne's Revenge*," Blackbeard insisted.

"I suppose my furry friends are welcome, too," Bonnet hinted, motioning toward Como and Cooper.

Blackbeard rubbed his black beard before answering. "They can come if they don't cause trouble."

"Are ye sure that's wise, Captain?" the cook named Cookie asked. "Don't ye remember the legend? Only black cats are lucky. Maybe Stede's crew is right. Perhaps he is a bad omen."

For a moment Cooper thought Blackbeard was going to agree with his cook. Stede must have been thinking the same thing. He promised to keep the animals under control.

"Very well," Blackbeard agreed at last. "But remember, they better not cause any trouble. I already have a mouser though, so the cat will have to share Tuffy's duties."

"Tuffy is the only mouser we need. She's a pirate cat and a trusted member of the crew," Cookie objected.

"Cooper is a wonderful mouser, too," Stede promised.

His words made Cooper's stomach churn with worry. He wasn't so sure he was as good as Stede thought.

"No one is replacing Tuffy. She's the only ship's cat I have ever approved of and like ye said, she's a member of the crew," Blackbeard said.

"He will have to prove himself worthy to be on *Queen Anne's Revenge*," Cookie continued.

"We shall see how good of a mouser Cooper turns out to be," Blackbeard added.

Stede slowly nodded as he glanced at his former crew. It seemed clear that he no longer held any sort of power over the pirates. Blackbeard's offer to make him co-captain was more of a formality than a real position. After all, Blackbeard was obviously in complete control of the whole group.

"Well," Como whispered. "I guess this means we are headed back to your old ship."

"I guess so," Cooper muttered.

He wondered what kind of cat Tuffy was and whether this bad omen thing was true. Maybe the pirates were right. Could he be the reason they were unsuccessful in capturing the prize ship? Did he bring bad luck to the *La Concorde* when Blackbeard captured it five moons ago? If so, what could he do to change his luck?

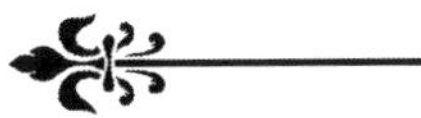 CHAPTER TWO 

Treasure Hunt

Palm trees swayed in the midday breeze as Cooper trotted swiftly over the sandy beach. His green eyes scanned the lush tropical bushes on the edge of the beach hoping to spy his little furry friend. Ever since Captain Stede Bonnet had let Cooper and Como loose on the island this morning, the two friends had been playing a hiding game.

Being a spider monkey, Como had the advantage of hiding among the tall, crooked trees, but Cooper's sense of smell was strong. It didn't take him long to locate Como in a beautiful, red-flowered tropical plant.

Using his hunting skills, Cooper slowly crept forward. Very carefully, he eased his way closer until he could see a tiny bit of Como's brown tail twitching slightly behind some green stalks.

"Found you!" Cooper shouted.

The little brown spider monkey jumped in fright. When he popped his head out of the bush, he was wearing a big grin.

"You scared me, Coop. It's my turn to count to ten while you find a place to hide."

Excitement flooded over Cooper as Como covered his eyes with his hands and started to count.

"One . . . two . . . three . . ."

Cooper looked around, trying to decide where to go hide. He spotted a rock further up the beach that appeared to be a good spot. Glancing back at Como, he noticed the sneaky little monkey was peeping through his fingers at him.

"Hey, no peeping!" Cooper protested. "You're going to have to start over."

Groaning, Como started counting again, this time with his back to Cooper so he couldn't see him. Cooper scampered off to his chosen hiding place. He slipped behind the rock and skidded to a halt just as something big lunged at him.

Terrified, Cooper tripped on his own tail as he attempted to run away. The huge beast came closer, snapping its wide jaws full of sharp teeth. Cooper quickly got up and ran back onto the sandy beach.

"I found you, Coop!" Como shouted as he ran toward him. "You didn't even try to hide."

"Watch out, Como, there's a beast behind the rock."

The dark green beast clawed its way onto the beach just as Como came to a stop beside Cooper. Its yellow eyes on either side of its long snout glared at them.

"That's a crocodilly!" Como yelled. "Run, Coop!"

Both friends took off. Behind them, the crocodile gave a little chase, but with its short legs it didn't go far. Once they were a safe distance away, Cooper and Como stopped running.

"Whew! I thought that crocodilly was going to eat us. His teeth looked sharp," Cooper said.

Tired and out of breath, they watched the crocodile retreat to the rock. They were surprised when someone spoke to them.

"What are the two of you up to?"

Turning around, Cooper saw Tuffy standing behind them. The solid black cat was older than Cooper and spoke with authority. Although Cooper and Como had only been around her for a couple of days, it was clear she was still studying them as if they were going through some sort of test.

Honestly, Cooper was afraid of Tuffy. As if her name wasn't intimidating enough, she was missing her left eye. This added to her mysterious character.

"We were playing a hiding game," Como explained.

"Playing?" Tuffy blurted out. "Well, you better come with me. Captain Blackbeard called the pirates together. They spotted another ship coming into the lagoon. He has ordered the men to prepare to take the ship."

"Do you think Blackbeard will keep this ship, too?" Como asked.

Before Tuffy could reply, another cat came running up to them from the pirate encampment. The young she-cat was calling for Tuffy. Surprised, Cooper stared at the new arrival, wondering where she came from. She had black fur with white on her paws.

"What is it, Prissy?" Tuffy asked.

"The pirate cook is looking for you."

"Alright, I'm coming."

"Where did she come from?" Como asked Tuffy as the little monkey pointed to the black and white cat.

"Prissy arrived on the island shortly after the two of you scampered off. Blackbeard's quartermaster, William Howard, brought her ashore from one of the captured ships," Tuffy explained.

"I'm the ship's cat for the *Adventure*," Prissy said.

"Is Blackbeard keeping this new ship?" Como wanted to know.

"Possibly. I overheard Captain tell Cookie last night that he plans to go after the ship Stede Bonnet let escape. Having a large fleet of ships would make it much easier to capture it. Now come with me. We will be staying here on the island with Cookie, of course, but we need to be prepared for anything," Tuffy informed them.

The black cat retraced her steps to the pirate encampment. Prissy, Como, and Cooper followed her. In a way, she was like their captain and they were her obedient crew.

While they walked, Cooper thought about Captain Blackbeard's plans. Over the past few days, the pirate crews had trapped two ships that had ventured into the wide lagoon. The ships had no doubt expected to anchor at Turneffe Island to restock on food and freshwater or maybe even careen their ships by cleaning the barnacles off the bottom.

Although Blackbeard decided to keep both prize ships, he was particularly pleased with the first one they captured. It was an eighty-ton logwood-cutting sloop called the *Adventure*. Blackbeard put the captain of the ship, David Herriot, under arrest in the hold of the *La Concorde*. Apparently, Prissy had belonged to the crew.

Both ships had been carrying cargo, though neither of them held any gold or jewels. Most of it was logwood and barrels of sugar and cotton, but the pirates were more interested in the navigational tools and the tools used for ship repair.

Now that Blackbeard had captured a third ship, Cooper couldn't help but wonder what kind of cargo it held. Perhaps this ship would be carrying the gold and jewels the pirates wanted the most. He also worried about the other ship cats. It hadn't occurred to him that the captured ships would naturally have cats of their own.

Beyond the rolling waves splashing onto the white sand, Cooper could see the pirate ship *La Concorde* heading out to meet the new arrival. The *Revenge* remained anchored near the shore with the other two prize ships anchored on either side of her. All the captive crews were prisoners below the decks.

This new ship coming into the lagoon was much smaller than the *La Concorde*, or as Tuffy called it, *Queen Anne's Revenge*. According to her, Blackbeard had renamed his flagship shortly after he transferred Cooper to another ship five moons ago.

Cooper wasn't sure why Blackbeard renamed the ship, but its new name suited it well. *Queen Anne's Revenge* sounded more like the grand lady she was; a true queen of the sea.

By the time Tuffy, Prissy, Como, and Cooper were under the makeshift tent Cookie had set up on the beach, the pirate ship was firing off their cannons. A black flag flapped in the breeze at the top of the mast.

Most of the pirates had gone with Captain Blackbeard to engage with the trapped ship, though a small number of them were guarding the prisoners on the other two prize ships. Only Cookie, Stede Bonnet, and a young lad named JJ Brooks were still on the island.

"What in the heavens have ye got now?" Cookie asked Stede as he approached the tent.

Stede carried a bright red object in his arms as he struggled to drag a fishing net behind him. Cooper realized the object was a sort of bird though it was a lot bigger and more colorful than the chickens he was familiar with on the ship. Having never seen a bird so big and beautiful before, Cooper stared in awe at the creature. Apparently, he wasn't the only one who had never seen one.

"What kind of bird is that?" JJ wanted to know with a laugh. "It's certainly not a chicken!"

"It's called a scarlet macaw. They are relatives to their smaller parrot cousins. I have read about them in my books. Isn't she gorgeous?" Bonnet replied.

"Just what do ye plan to do with it?" Cookie asked.

"Keep it, of course."

"We are pirates, not animal keepers."

"I am not just a pirate. I am an explorer and a collector of exotic things. This macaw is exotic, don't ye think?"

Cookie shook his head while JJ sat down on an old barrel. "We'll see what Blackbeard has to say about that bird."

More cannon fire echoed in the distance. The pirates' conversation grew serious as Stede walked over to where the pirates kept the cages of chickens. He located the empty one Cooper and Como slept in and put the scarlet macaw inside. Meanwhile, Tuffy moved closer to where JJ sat. The young pirate reached down to stroke Tuffy's black fur while Cookie argued with Stede about whether Blackbeard would keep or burn the now captured ship in the lagoon.

Cooper listened for a while until he realized Como was no longer sitting beside him. Startled that his friend was missing, Cooper looked around the encampment. His gaze lingered for a second on Prissy, who was sitting nearby. The she-cat seemed to be observing the pirates as if she was afraid of them.

For a moment, Cooper's mind slipped back to last fall when Blackbeard's fleet had captured his ship. He remembered how scared he had been. Prissy was probably feeling the same way, though Cooper reasoned that she didn't have to worry. With her black fur she would bring luck to the pirates.

Sighing, Cooper continued to search the camp with his green eyes. He finally spotted Como over by their cage poking his little arm between the wooden bars. Seconds later, Como jerked back as the scarlet macaw made a grab for his arm with her hooked beak.

"Hold it, birdy! That's my arm you're trying to bite," Como exclaimed as Cooper hurried over to where they were.

The scarlet macaw fluttered her large red wings. As she did so, Cooper realized the tops of her wings were red, but the middle part was yellow and the tips were a dark blue.

"If I wanted to bite you, I would have pulled out your fur. I'm warning you. Stay away," the macaw threatened.

"I just wanted to touch your pretty tail feathers," Como said.

"Don't try it. I have had a bad enough day as it is."

"Why?"

"Why do you think?" the macaw snapped sarcastically. "I was minding my own business, trying to find my treasure, when this thing fell on top of me."

"What thing?"

"Just leave her alone, Como," Cooper urged, sensing the bird wasn't in a good mood.

Como ignored him. "You mean the fishing net?"

"I really don't know what it was. Who are you anyway?"

"I'm Como and this is my friend Cooper. He's a ship's cat. Do you have a name?"

The bird cocked her head to one side so they could see the bare white around her small hazel-colored eye. "What sort of question is that? Of course, I have a name. It's Marisol."

"Nice to meet you, Marisol! Now what's this about a lost treasure?" Como continued.

At this point, Cooper tried to pull his friend away. "Don't pay attention to Como. He has a hard time controlling his excitement. I'm sorry Captain Bonnet captured you, Marisol."

"Can you help me get out of here?" Marisol asked.

"I might could open the latch . . ." Como began.

"Are you crazy?" Cooper blurted out. "If Captain Bonnet sees you, we will be in big trouble."

"I can probably do it when they aren't looking," Como argued.

"Forget breaking me out right now," Marisol interrupted. "Can the two of you go find my treasure? I had just found it when that man tossed the net on me."

"We can try," Como agreed. "Tell us how to get to where you were when Captain Bonnet caught you."

Cooper wasn't so sure he wanted to go on this mission, as Como was already calling it, but Marisol seemed relieved they were going to help her. She excitedly told them which way to go and described her treasure in detail so they knew what they were looking for.

Marisol said her grandfather had given her the treasure and since he died last fall, it was very important to her. It sounded like the object resembled a small bird and was something she could wear around her neck.

Acting quickly but quietly, Como and Cooper slipped away from the pirate encampment unnoticed by either Tuffy, Prissy, or the humans. They seemed to be too busy watching Blackbeard bring the prize ship closer to shore.

As he trotted over the sand behind his friend, Cooper began to feel nervous again. His fear only deepened as he and Como left the safety of the beach and started a trail through the tropical bushes. He kept a lookout for any crocodiles lurking in the ferns.

The scenery was beautiful. Flowers of red, yellow, purple, and orange dotted the forest of crooked trees. Overhead, fuzzy brown balls hung in the palm trees. Having never been on any islands before, Cooper was fascinated by all the strange plants and trees.

Knowing that Como had lived on an island prior to his capture, Cooper decided to ask him about these weird things. Como happily explained the names of a variety of plants and told him that the odd-looking trees were seaside trees called mangroves.

"I hoped this island had bananas, but I don't see any banana trees. I love eating bananas, they are delicious! You would love them too, Coop. All you do is peel back the yellow outside. The inside is sweet and soft to eat. They are so much better than those coconuts," Como said as he pointed at the fuzzy brown balls in the palm trees. "Coconuts are hard to crack and once you get to the white meat—that's what they call the fruit inside—it's sweet but a bit chewy. I always liked the juice more than the meat. It's creamy."

He continued to talk about other kinds of fruit he enjoyed back on his home island. Cooper listened and learned as they trudged through the mangrove forest. Soon they came to a small clearing which gave way to a pool of water. It appeared to be the same location Marisol the macaw told them about.

"Do you see that rotten stump over on the other side of the pool?" Como asked. "It has to be where Marisol's treasure is."

Cooper nodded in agreement as Como started to run around the left side of the pool of water. Trying to keep up with him, Cooper zigzagged past bushes and rocks. Surprisingly, Como was a lot faster than he looked for such a little fellow.

The two friends were nearly at the old rotten stump when something big and blue swooped down from the sky. Startled, Cooper instinctively ducked to avoid whatever it was.

"What in the world was that?" Como exclaimed as he stopped in his tracks.

"I don't know," Cooper muttered.

Looking around, Cooper realized there wasn't anything blue on the ground or anywhere else nearby. Astonished, he briefly wondered if he had been seeing things, but quickly pushed that idea away as he remembered how Como had seen it, too.

Suddenly, another flash of blue seemingly fell from the sky yet again, though this time Cooper got a good look at it before it disappeared for the second time.

"I think it's a bird, Como."

"A bird? It's too big."

"Not really. Think about it. Marisol is a big bird."

"Coop, you're a genius! I bet it was another macaw. Where did it fly off to?" Como asked as he started looking up at the palm trees.

"I don't know, but we can't go looking for it. We are supposed to be finding Marisol's treasure, remember?"

"That's right!"

Cooper grinned as his furry friend hurriedly jumped over to the rotten stump. He had noticed on the first day he met Como how the little monkey seemed easily distracted. It was one of those things Como really needed to work on.

Thinking about this, Cooper suddenly wondered what things he might need to work on himself. For one thing, he certainly needed to work on his fear.

"Look! I found it!" Como shouted as he reached under a big root at the base of the rotten stump. He pulled out a bird-shaped, clay object with a string and held it high for Cooper to see. "Isn't it so—"

Before Como could finish his sentence, the blue macaw swooped through the air. Something white fell from the sky and plopped on top of Como's head as the macaw landed on one of the fern-like branches of a palm tree.

"Eww! That birdy pooped on me," Como gasped as he touched his head and looked at the white mess.

Cooper let out a meow of laughter. He was still laughing when the blue macaw took to the air again, this time flying low enough to snatch the string of the clay bird out of Como's hand. The macaw flew up to the nearest palm tree, but the string must not have been secure in its beak. To Cooper's horror, the treasure fell into some tropical bushes not far from where they stood. Thankfully, the bush seemed to protect the clay bird from breaking.

Reacting quickly, Cooper ran out to get the treasure. He managed to successfully grab it as the blue macaw swooped through the air toward him. Not sure what to do, Cooper instinctively flopped down on top of the clay bird to keep the macaw from stealing it again.

The blue macaw landed on a large rock. "Give me that treasure!"

"No way," Como shouted back as he joined Cooper.

"I must get it back. It belongs to a friend of mine."

Cooper glanced at Como and then back at the macaw. "What's

your friend's name?" he asked.

"Marisol."

"We know Marisol. She told us where to find her treasure," Como said as he picked a leaf off a nearby plant.

The little spider monkey went over to the pool of water. He dipped the leaf into the pool and used it to wipe the poop off his furry head.

"Where is Marisol? Why didn't she come here herself?" the macaw wanted to know.

"Captain Bonnet captured Marisol. He's a pirate."

Como explained how he and Cooper were sailing with the pirates. He then went into more detail about Marisol's situation. At first the blue macaw didn't believe it, but after they answered a few more of his questions he slowly seemed to trust them.

By the end of the conversation, the blue macaw revealed more about his friendship with Marisol. Although his flock of birds were all blue, yellow, and green like him, he spent a lot of time with Marisol and several other kinds of birds. His name was Marco.

"What are we waiting for? We must help Marisol escape," Marco said at last.

"We?" Como asked.

Marco tilted his blue head so they could see the white around his eye. "If we all work together, we can set her free. Come on, I'll follow you back to the beach."

Como picked up the clay bird by Cooper's paws. He slipped the string over Cooper's head so that the bird dangled against his furry chest.

"Why are you giving it to me?" Cooper asked. "Don't you think it's safer for you to wear it, Como?"

"Are you kidding? You know how clumsy I am."

"But I bring bad luck, remember?"

"I don't believe in bad luck."

Without another word, the little monkey led the way through the mangrove forest while Marco flew above them. Eventually, the three of them made it back to the sandy beach. Right away, Cooper noticed an enormous gathering. Among the couple hundred pirates, another group of men stood nearby wearing ropes around their hands. Cooper guessed Blackbeard's crew had captured these men from the prize ship.

Knowing the pirates had searched the other two prize ships for gold and jewels, Cooper assumed they were making sure the crew wasn't keeping gold in their pockets. Luckily, the pirates seemed too busy patting down the newly captured men to notice Como, Cooper, and Marco. Acting quickly, the three of them approached the stack of cages where the chickens were. Marisol was thrilled to see them.

"You found my treasure and Marco, too!" she exclaimed.

"I've been looking all over for you, Marisol," Marco said. "We're going to get you out of this cage."

Suddenly, something heavy fell from the sky and covered them. Fear engulfed Cooper as he immediately sent up a prayer for the Mighty Creator's help. He realized the heavy thing on top of them was a net. Unfortunately, no matter how much Cooper, Como, and Marco struggled to get free, it was too heavy to lift.

"What do we have here?" asked a voice above them.

Looking up through the net, Cooper saw that the voice belonged to Captain Stede Bonnet. The pirate captain wore a big smile on his face as he slowly lifted a corner of the net.

"Hold still, macaw, or ye will injure ye wings. Ye are such a beautiful blue macaw! I think I'll keep ye as well," Stede said as he attempted to hold Marco still.

"Captain Bonnet, Blackbeard wants to talk to ye," another voice said as he walked up. Cooper recognized the pirate as young JJ Brooks. "What are ye doing with the net?"

"This blue macaw flew into camp. I'm going to add it to my collection. Aren't these blue, green, and yellow feathers splendid?"

JJ chuckled as he shook his head. He lifted the other corner of the net while Stede fought with Marco. The blue macaw put up a good fight, but eventually Stede succeeded in getting him into the cage with Marisol. Meanwhile, JJ released Como. Cooper expected the pirate to free him as well, but at the last moment JJ scooped him up.

Meowing in protest, Cooper squirmed in his grasp. The young pirate grabbed the clay bird still hanging around his neck. As soon as JJ slipped it off his neck, he let Cooper go.

"What is it?" Stede asked as he looked over JJ's shoulder at Marisol's treasure.

The young pirate studied the clay bird in his hand while Cooper stared up at him. A sickening feeling settled in his stomach. His bad luck had struck again!

"I think it's a clay flute," JJ said as he put it up to his mouth.

To Cooper's surprise, a whistle sound came out of the little clay bird. He glanced at Como and the macaws, who all seemed just as surprised as he was. Marisol looked like she might faint.

"Actually, it's an ocarina," Stede told JJ. "The ancient people of Belize made these flutes in shapes of animals. This one looks like a bird, maybe even a macaw. I have read about them in my books."

JJ looked at Stede as if he were talking crazy. "Whatever it is, I wonder how the cat got it."

"I told ye Cooper is a smart cat. Anyway, I'll add it to my collection of exotic things."

"Nay, I found it first so I'm going to keep it."

Cooper felt miserable as JJ walked away with the little clay bird. It was all his fault. Why wasn't he able to protect Marisol's treasure? Did he even try hard enough or did his fear get in the way? He had to do something to get it back, but how?

 CHAPTER THREE 

Revenge

The last few days had been a whirlwind of events for Cooper and his friends. Captain Blackbeard's interrogation of the crew of the third captured ship had ended in an enraged dispute with its captain. It got so far out of hand that Blackbeard ordered his men to remove all the valuables from the ship and burn it.

While his crew followed orders, a fourth ship sailed into the lagoon. Soon, the pirates had overtaken it as well. At first Cooper feared that Blackbeard would torture or maybe even kill the growing number of captives, but he didn't. According to Tuffy, Blackbeard had threatened and injured his captives, but had never killed anyone in the two years Tuffy had been with the fearsome captain.

After a few more days on Turneffe Island, Blackbeard was ready to seek revenge on the captain who outsmarted Stede Bonnet. With *Queen Anne's Revenge* leading the way, the new fleet of ships set sail for the last known location of the *Protestant Caesar.*

Just as he promised, Captain Blackbeard allowed Stede Bonnet to co-captain the *Queen*, or at least pretend to be co-captain. Stede took his new position seriously as he ordered the men around. Like his previous crew, these pirates were clearly getting annoyed with him, but with Blackbeard tolerating it, they didn't dare complain. None of them said a word about Cooper, Como, and the macaws coming aboard either.

For Cooper, this new journey was bittersweet. It had been five moons since he last set his paws on this ship. So much had changed, he barely recognized it.

Besides the pirates being in charge, Cooper now had to share the mouser duties with Tuffy, who seemed more qualified than Cooper. This was why Cooper was down in the ship's galley where the pirates cooked and ate their meals instead of on deck watching Como do tricks in the sails. If he was going to survive on this ship, he had to practice his hunting skills.

Cooper carefully eased himself around the brick fire pit where Cookie cooked the meals. The brick around the fire pit and the large bucket of sand nearby kept the fire from burning up the wooden ship, but it also attracted mice. Since Cookie hadn't sent Cooper or Tuffy to stalk the galley, Cooper doubted any mice were there. Still, it gave him a chance to practice being a silent hunter.

"What are you doing?" asked a voice behind him.

Turning around, Cooper saw Tuffy standing at the bottom of the stairs which led up to the main deck. Embarrassed, he tried to come up with a good reason for his behavior, but couldn't come up with anything without lying.

"I—I was just practicing my hunting skills," he muttered.

Tuffy tilted her head to one side as she studied Cooper with her single green eye. Her silence drove Cooper crazy. He figured she thought he wasn't capable of being a mouser if he felt the need to practice. Finally, she spoke.

"Well, you will have to put those skills to good use. It's about time for us to check on the barrels down in the hold. I figured we could start with the food barrels and later move on to the barrels of rum and brandy. What's your opinion? After all, this was your ship."

"Okay."

Tuffy narrowed her eye as if she were debating whether to question Cooper further. "Alright, let's go."

Cooper followed the one-eyed, black cat through the doorway and into the next room where the crew slept. The two of them passed rows of sailcloth hammocks hanging from the wooden boards of the ceiling. Unlike the galley, this room was so dark Cooper had to allow his green eyes time to adjust. Luckily, cats were naturally better hunters in the dark.

Before long they came to the end of the sleeping quarters. Another staircase led down into the hold of the ship where the pirates kept the barrels of food, water, and liquors. This was also where the former captain of the *La Concorde* had kept the fine linens that he eventually traded for Africans.

Later, the captain held the Africans prisoner down there. Cooper could still remember how packed the room was and how many rats lived down in the hold with the humans.

As Tuffy started down the stairs, Cooper felt an uneasiness come over him. He shivered, partly in fear but also in hopes to shake the worry building in his chest. The feeling wasn't new to him. In fact, he had always felt this way when he used to go down into the belly of the *La Concorde* after many Africans and Frenchmen had gotten sick and died.

There was something eerie about the deepest, darkest deck of the ship. Perhaps it was the way the ship creaked and groaned as it shifted its weight over the waves of the sea. Every little noise seemed much louder down here. It almost felt haunted.

"What are you waiting for?" Tuffy asked from the bottom of the stairs as she looked up at Cooper.

"I'm coming," Cooper said as he took a deep breath and descended the stairs.

"You seem uneasy. I know you feel uncomfortable being on a pirate ship, but I'm here to help, not make things difficult. Be honest with me, what's going on?"

Cooper briefly debated what to do. Could he trust Tuffy or was this a test? She seemed to be genuinely concerned.

"There is something about this place," Cooper began. "I know you think I'm crazy, but it feels spooky."

"Is it the room or you?" Tuffy asked as Cooper looked down at his paws. When he didn't respond she continued, "I have heard the crew making comments about you being a bad omen and I'm sure you have heard them, too. I don't think you're a bad omen, Cooper, I just think you have an issue believing in yourself."

"I'm trying."

"I know you are. The fact is, you have a choice to make. You can choose to believe in this bad omen or you can choose to make your own path. Now, let's split up so we can cover more space. I'll go ask Henrietta and Rooney if they've noticed any rats gnawing at the hull."

"Henrietta and Rooney? Who are they?" Cooper asked.

"They are the ship's chickens. Of course, we have more than just them, but the others are food for the pirates. Henrietta and I have sailed together for a long time. She's a wise old hen. Rooney is our main rooster. He joined the crew a couple of moons before you did."

Cooper recalled having chickens onboard before, but he didn't think they had names. Although he didn't want to split up, Cooper didn't argue. He watched Tuffy's black silhouette disappear into the shadows. Taking a deep breath, he slowly made his way to the center of the ship where the pirates kept the heaviest barrels and crates to help stabilize the ship in the water.

In the distance, Cooper could hear the scratching of the rats and the squeaks of mice. Instinct started to kick in as he focused his attention on the sounds, attempting to single one of them out. Eventually, he located a single mouse nibbling on some rope.

Going into hunting mode, Cooper unsheathed his claws. He crouched down to the floor and inched closer to the unsuspecting mouse. Once he was within killing distance, he shook his haunches and pounced. As soon as Cooper's claws trapped the mouse, he quickly bit its throat before it could squeak.

"Hello down there!" shouted a voice from the stairs. "Where are you, Coop? I have some news I think you will be interested in."

Recognizing Como's voice, Cooper picked up the dead mouse in his jaws and carried it back to the stairway. The little brown monkey was standing on the last step waiting for him.

"Congratulations, Coop! You got one of those squeaks."

Cooper dropped the dead mouse at his paws. "Thanks. What's going on?"

"The *Protestant Caesar* has been spotted."

Before Cooper could respond, Tuffy walked up to them carrying three mice by their tails. The one-eyed, black cat dropped them so she could speak.

"Has Captain Blackbeard called a meeting yet?" she asked.

"Sort of. Blackbeard told the crew we should be within firing distance within an hour. He also ordered them to slow *Queen Anne's Revenge* down and to call the other ships together," Como said.

"Does that mean we're going into battle?" Cooper asked.

"Yes, but there is no need to worry," Tuffy replied. "Blackbeard prepares for battle, even though he prefers to scare potential prize ships in hopes that they will surrender. Otherwise, we would never get anything out of the ships. Come on, let's take these mice upstairs and go see what's happening up on deck."

Tuffy picked up her fresh kill and headed up the stairs. Humiliated by how fast she outhunted him, Cooper grabbed the dead mouse with his teeth and joined Como as the two of them scampered behind her. On the second floor, they dropped the mice in a corner of the sleeping quarters where Tuffy slept. The pirates didn't allow Cooper and Como to sleep with the crew. They had to sleep in the captain's cabin with the macaws and Stede Bonnet.

With the mice put away for supper, Cooper and Como followed Tuffy through the galley and up the second flight of stairs to the main deck. Cooper had to squint to see in the bright sunlight. The first thing he noticed was a large pile of swords and guns in the center of the deck.

"What are those pirates doing?" Como asked as he pointed to the crew who were moving around on the deck like wild men.

"They are getting things ready for battle. There is plenty to do before we are ready to challenge the *Protestant Caesar*. Looks like Captain is about to speak. Let's get closer so we can hear him," Tuffy explained.

As they approached the center of the deck, Cooper could see that the other ships had come within shouting distance of the *Queen Anne's Revenge*. Blackbeard climbed the stairs to the quarterdeck which was above the large captain's cabin. With a brass speaking trumpet in his hand, the tall, bearded pirate addressed his own crew and the crews of the *Revenge, Adventure, Land of Promise,* and *Adventure II* who were listening at their ship's railings.

"Listen up, men," Blackbeard yelled in his trumpet. "We're nearing Honduras. As many of ye already know, the ship anchored there is the *Protestant Caesar*. I don't want to damage it so make sure the cannon fire is minimal. Keep ye weapons ready though because ye never know how they will react. Remember, this is revenge."

One of the pirates from the prize ship *Adventure* waved his three-cornered hat in the air as he tried to get Blackbeard's attention. Cooper instantly recognized the man who always wore a bright red shirt. Blackbeard had made him the new captain of the *Adventure*.

"What is it, Israel?" Blackbeard asked.

Israel grabbed his own speaking trumpet so Blackbeard could hear him. "Captain, what are we supposed to do with the men that we captured at Turneffe Island? I have about twenty on the *Adventure*. They haven't caused any trouble yet, but I'm not sure we can trust them when we go into battle."

"I guess now is a good time to see where their loyalties are," Blackbeard replied. "All of ye who came from the captured ships have a choice to make. Ye can either join us or choose to remain prisoners. By joining our ranks ye must follow orders, swear the oath we have all taken, and swear to fight until death if necessary.

As pirates, ye will get the same portion of captured treasure as an average crewmate. If ye wish to remain prisoners, then we will chain ye up and lock ye in the hold of the ship ye are currently on until I decide what to do with ye. What will it be?"

There was some commotion on each of the five ships as the captives made up their minds. Surprisingly, the majority of the men decided to join the ranks of pirates. Those who clearly didn't want to become pirates were bound with ropes and swiftly taken below deck as Captain Blackbeard had promised.

After giving a few more orders on how to trap the *Protestant Caesar*, Blackbeard descended the stairs of the quarterdeck. He was immediately approached by his co-captain, Stede Bonnet, who was trying to talk him out of attacking the *Protestant Caesar*.

Blackbeard dismissed the cowardly pirate with a flick of his hand. "Stede, I told ye at Turneffe Island what my plans were. Captain Wyer isn't going to get the upper hand. He crossed the line when he attacked ye and the crew of the *Revenge*. The *Protestant Caesar* must pay. This will teach them not to mess with pirates."

"But it wasn't all their fault, Edward. I misjudged how close they were and probably made a few other bad decisions. What will ye do if they come after us again?" Stede asked.

"They can't outgun five ships and seven hundred men."

"Can ye at least send the other ships ahead of us so we don't have to fight them first?"

Looking at the shocked faces of his crew, Blackbeard grabbed Stede's arm. "Don't start talking crazy. Let's talk privately in my cabin. Get back to work, men. When I return, ye better be ready for battle."

Both captains walked toward the great cabin at the rear of the ship while the crew got to work. Captain Blackbeard held open the cabin door for Stede as Tuffy spoke to Cooper and Como.

"Come on, let's go with Captain."

Cooper glanced at his little monkey friend. Como shrugged his furry shoulders before scampering behind Tuffy. Not wanting to be alone with the pirates and their sharp swords, Cooper ran to catch up with them. Thankfully, he managed to slip through the crack in the door just as it was closing.

The great cabin consisted of a medium-sized room with smaller rooms off to each side. Another tiny room stood off to the right where the pirates relieved themselves. This main area had a large oak desk with a beautifully carved, straight-backed chair behind it.

Like most ships, this was where the captain kept his navigational tools, maps, and personal weapons. Since the *Queen Anne's Revenge* was much bigger than most ships, her captain's cabin allowed Stede to share the space with Blackbeard.

Cooper, Como, and the macaws had been staying with Stede in the room on the right beside the tiny room or the head, as the pirates called it. Although their room was smaller than the one Blackbeard slept in, it was still a lot more comfortable than the stuffy sleeping quarters down in the hold.

Stede continued to talk aimlessly about the *Protestant Caesar*, but Blackbeard was no longer listening. The pirate captain had unlocked a large wooden chest sitting against the back wall of bookcases. Unlike the *Revenge*, these bookcases held a variety of tools intermingled with a few books. So far Stede had been unsuccessful in convincing Blackbeard to fill the whole shelf with his collection of books that the pirates packed in crates and transferred from the *Revenge*.

Once the chest was open, Blackbeard pulled out some sort of black leather belt, six small guns, and a piece of folded black material. Cooper watched in amazement as Blackbeard slipped the belt over his head so it hung from his right shoulder to his left side. As he slid the six guns into the leather straps of the belt, he finally interrupted Stede Bonnet.

"Will ye stop talking and start getting ready? Put ye bandolier on and fill ye flintlock pistols with gunpowder and lead shot," Blackbeard said.

"Ye didn't fill ye pistols," Stede pointed out.

"I don't need to. My guns are always ready to fire. Ye never know when ye might have to settle an argument with an unruly crew of scoundrels."

Bonnet's eyes widened in shock. He silently went to his room and came back with a bandolier belt like Blackbeard's. When he returned, he left his door open.

"Let's go tell Marisol and Marco what's happening," Como whispered to Cooper.

The little brown monkey quickly entered the small side room. Cooper looked over at Tuffy as she jumped up on a chair to watch the pirates. Following his friend, Cooper entered the side room where he could hear Como talking to the macaws.

Unfortunately, Marco had injured his right wing when he tried to escape Stede Bonnet's net back at Turneffe Island. Stede and Cookie had bandaged his wing to keep him from hurting it worse. Thankfully, the blue-feathered macaw was doing much better now and could move his wing some.

Between Marco's injury and Marisol's missing treasure, the macaws decided they didn't want Como and Cooper to help them escape. As far as they knew, the ocarina flute was still in the possession of JJ Brooks. The problem was JJ and his father, Joseph, were no longer on the *Queen Anne's Revenge.*

Tuffy had explained to Cooper and Como that Blackbeard was friends with Joseph Brooks and had asked him and JJ to move to the *Adventure* which was now under the command of Israel Hands.

According to Tuffy, Israel was short tempered and determined to prove he was ready to be a leader. Most likely, Blackbeard wanted his friend Joseph to keep an eye on Israel.

"Hello, Cooper," Marisol said as Cooper walked up to the bird cages in the back corner of the room. "Como was just telling us about the prize ship and the possibility of a battle."

Cooper looked up at Como, who had climbed on top of the small, wood-framed bed beside the bird cages. To his surprise, the little brown monkey had a sneaky grin on his face.

"Did I miss something?" Cooper asked.

"Tell him your idea, Como," Marco suggested from his wooden cage above Marisol's.

"I'm sure the captain of the *Protestant Caesar* will give in to the pirates. I know I would if I saw five ships full of bloodthirsty pirates coming after me," Como said.

"Hurry up and spit it out," Marco interrupted.

"Hold it, birdy. I'm getting to it," Como continued. "At some point, the pirates will leave our ship to steal theirs. When they do, we can go get Marisol's treasure."

"But her treasure is on another ship," Cooper pointed out.

"We will just have to go over there and get it."

"How?"

"I don't know yet, but I'll think of something. In the meantime, let's go back outside where we can watch the pirates," Como said as he hopped down from the bed.

The little spider monkey reached for the latch on Marisol's cage. He slid it open and climbed up to Marco's cage above hers.

"What are you doing?" Marisol asked the little monkey.

"I figured it would be a good idea to open your cages just in case you need to get out. Coop and I might need your help later."

"You can count on us!" Marco squawked.

Marisol flapped her pretty, red feathers in excitement. "We'll be waiting for your signal."

Cooper and Como returned to the map room just in time to see Captain Blackbeard and Captain Bonnet going out the door to the main deck. Tuffy was right on their heels. Acting quickly, the two friends ran to catch up with them.

Once they were out on the deck, Cooper noticed Blackbeard walking up the stairs to the quarterdeck. He was wearing a long red coat and a black three-cornered hat with a feather in it. The pirate captain had tucked all six flintlock pistols into his leather bandolier and had a long silver sword hanging at his left side.

At the top of the stairs, the fearsome pirate captain pulled a spyglass out of his coat pocket. He held it up to his right eye as he studied the horizon. Moments later, he was calling out to his quartermaster, William Howard, who was the second in command of the ship. Unlike Stede Bonnet's madeup position, William's crewmates voted him in as their quartermaster.

"William, send word to Philip Morton to load the cannons below deck. Tell him to wait for my signal to fire them."

"The gunner is already down there with several men, Captain, but I'll tell him," William said as he went down into the ship.

"Stede, tell the men to send the Death's Head up the mast," Blackbeard added to Stede Bonnet.

The cowardly Captain Bonnet tried to act as if he really had control as he strutted over to the nearest group of pirates. He self-consciously adjusted the collar of his long, light gray coat and tilted his three-cornered hat so the bright red feather curled just right.

"He thinks he's something special," Tuffy muttered as she shook her head. "If Captain Blackbeard didn't look after him, he would have already gotten himself killed."

"What's the Death's Head thing Blackbeard is talking about?" Cooper asked her.

"It's our flag. The pirates call it the Death's Head because it strikes fear in the hearts of all who see it. There is a picture of a human skull on the black cloth."

Sure enough, the pirates tied the black flag to a rope at the base of the tallest of the three masts in the center of the ship. Cooper remembered seeing Blackbeard taking the material out of his wooden chest earlier. Over the past five moons, Cooper had seen the pirates fly the black flag many times when they were attacking prize ships, but this was the first time he had heard them call it the Death's Head.

Soon, the black flag was flapping in the breeze at the top of the mast. A grinning skull stared down at them, causing chills to go down

Cooper's spine. Tuffy was right; the Death's Head did strike fear!

Pirates on the other ships began to send up their own flags. The crew of the *Revenge* flew a Death's Head on their main mast as well, but the other three captured ships sent solid red flags up their masts.

"Why are those ships flying red flags?" Como asked Tuffy.

"Blackbeard probably didn't have any extra Death's Head flags. It's common for pirates to substitute it with red or black material. A white flag signals a surrender."

Suddenly, Blackbeard gave a shout. Seconds later there was a loud boom followed by a violent shift of the *Queen Anne's Revenge*. Another series of booms followed the first as the ship shook beneath Cooper's orange paws.

Terrified, Cooper grasped the wooden deck with his claws. Como couldn't hold on to anything with his fingers. The sudden shift threw the little spider monkey against the ship's railing. Thankfully, he jumped right up.

"What was that?" Cooper gasped.

"Cannon fire," Tuffy answered, relaxing her own claws. "We should get off the deck. It will be dangerous out here."

"What is Blackbeard doing? Has he lost his mind?" Como asked as he pointed at the pirate captain.

Cooper's green eyes widened in surprise as he watched the fearsome pirate tuck pieces of cloth under his tricorn hat. Blackbeard then struck a match against a crate to light the slow-burning fuses. The flame caused a ring of smoke to circle his face and black beard, making him appear frightening.

"Blackbeard lights the fuses so when captains see him in their spyglass, they think he's wild and dangerous," Tuffy explained.

"I think he's crazy," Como said.

"You can say that again," Cooper added.

Tuffy chuckled. "Some pirates think he is. I have even heard some of his prisoners call him the devil. Personally, I admire him. There aren't many pirates who value human life. Most would murder their victims, but he always chooses to rough them up instead."

Another round of cannon fire echoed from at least two of the nearby ships. At first, Cooper thought the *Protestant Caesar* was firing back at them, but he quickly realized it was coming from the other ships in the pirate fleet.

"It's time for us to go. Come on," Tuffy said as she trotted across the deck and headed downstairs.

Cooper started to follow her when he noticed Como scampering off. The little monkey climbed up on top of a crate sitting at the back of the ship beside the quarterdeck's staircase. When he saw Cooper coming over, the sneaky monkey held up a spyglass.

"Como, put that back! You're going to get us in trouble," Cooper warned as he looked around to see if any of the pirates had seen him.

"Blackbeard isn't using it right now. I saw him lay it down while he was lighting those fuses. Jump up here, Coop. We can check this thing out."

Fear engulfed Cooper as he debated what to do. He glanced at the pirates who were running back and forth on the deck changing the positions of the sails. Captain Blackbeard was at the ship's helm, steering it in the right direction. With his hands firmly on the giant wheel and his eyes focused on their target, he was too busy to see the sneaky monkey.

In his mind, Cooper recalled what Tuffy had said to him earlier while they were hunting mice. Maybe she was right about him needing to choose his own path. Part of that involved learning to overcome his fear.

Trying to put his fear aside, Cooper shook his haunches and jumped up on the crate beside his friend. By now, Como was already holding the spyglass up to his eye.

"Goodness! These pirates are wasting their time and energy. We're so far from land, there is no way those cannons can reach the enemy ship," Como said.

Cooper meowed with laughter as he realized Como was holding the spyglass the wrong way. The spider monkey squinted into the large end of the instrument which made the land seem far away.

"Why are you laughing?" Como asked.

"No wonder you can't see. You're holding it backwards."

Como looked at the spyglass before flipping it around. "I knew that. I was just making sure you were paying attention."

"I think you have been around Captain Bonnet too long. His silly behavior must be rubbing off on you," Cooper said.

"I don't know about that, but his handsome looks certainly have rubbed off," he replied as he proudly stuck out his chest.

"You better hurry up before Blackbeard sees us."

The spider monkey peered through the small end of the spyglass. "It looks like the *Protestant Caesar* anchored right off the Honduran coast. Did I tell you about those nights before you came aboard when Captain Bonnet read his books aloud to me? One time he read about Honduras. The book said Honduras was a Spanish name for the depth of the water. I think it needs a different name. Yes, the water is very deep, probably deeper than most places, but the jungle is . . ."

"Como," Cooper interrupted him. "You're rambling again. Get back to what's going on now. You can tell me about the book later."

"Oh. Right. Back to the ship. I think it's a log-cutting ship. There is a huge pile of logs on the beach. Wait, they are leaving."

"Leaving? How can they sail away when we have them blocked in? Do they really think they can outrun a fleet of pirates?"

"Sorry, Coop. I didn't mean to say they were trying to sail away. Those sailors are leaving their ship. I can see a group of them climbing into a periauger boat. A bunch of the crew is already on the mainland. Want to see?"

"I can't hold it like you can."

"No problem. I'll hold it for you. Don't forget to close one of your eyes. It makes it easier to see."

Como held the spyglass up to Cooper's eye. Squinting, Cooper peered into it. To his surprise, the spyglass made it feel like he was almost on the *Protestant Caesar*.

Just like Como had said, the men appeared to be abandoning their ship. A white flag of surrender flew at the top of the mast. Several boatloads of men were already on the beach with the pile of freshly cut trees. Strangely, they looked like they were running away from the beach and into the thick forest of bushes and vines.

"Is that the jungle you mentioned?" Cooper asked as he studied the unusual forest.

Como took the spyglass back. "You guessed right, Coop. A jungle is a scary place. Lots of strange animals live in jungles, but the meanest are probably crocodillies and big jungle cats called jaguars. I hope we don't go ashore. I don't like jungles."

"How do you know about jungles if you were born on an island?"

"I learned it from Captain Bonnet. His books had a lot to say about the jungle. I figured any place with crocodillies and jaguars is a place I don't want to be."

"Those men must be desperate if they would rather face jungle cats and crocodillies instead of pirates," Cooper said as he caught a glimpse of someone coming toward them.

Panic raced through Cooper's mind as he realized it was Blackbeard. He urgently shook Como with his right paw to get his attention, but it was too late.

"Sneaky little rascal! Give me that spyglass," Blackbeard snarled as he snatched the instrument out of Como's furry hand.

Como said something to the pirate captain, but of course Blackbeard only heard a bunch of squeaky chatter.

"Don't talk back to me, ye mischievous monkey. Ye better not steal my stuff again. As for ye, Cooper, I think ye need to consider who ye hang out with," Blackbeard continued angrily. The pirate captain looked down at the spyglass in his hand and let out a sigh. "Why am I wasting my breath? Ye probably can't understand me."

Blackbeard opened the spyglass and looked at the *Protestant Caesar*. After a few moments, he slid the interlocking sections of the spyglass together and turned to his crew.

"Hold ye fire!" Blackbeard ordered his men. "They have abandoned their ship and are hiding like scared rabbits in the jungle foliage. Pull the ships around in a semi-circle so we can board the prize and take inventory."

The pirates cheered in excitement as they prepared to drop the anchor. Even Captain Blackbeard smiled as he put out the smoking fuses and slipped off the bandolier full of pistols. Seeing how pleased the fearsome pirate was, Cooper felt relieved. Maybe he had forgotten about Como stealing his spyglass.

"Well, I guess it's time to put my plan into motion," Como said.

"What plan?" Cooper asked, feeling a rush of fear come over him as he wondered what the sneaky monkey was going to do next.

"You'll see. Come on, we need to talk with Marco and Marisol."

Cooper watched the little monkey jump down to the deck. As he joined his friend, he couldn't stop worrying. Como's so-called plans hadn't been very successful lately. He hoped this one wouldn't make the pirates mad.

 CHAPTER FOUR 

Walking The Plank

Gray clouds and drizzling rain had made things difficult for the pirates, but it didn't stop them from plundering the *Protestant Caesar*. For three days, the pirates had been scouring every inch of the prize ship and transferring anything of value to the other five ships in the fleet. Meanwhile, the crew of the *Protestant Caesar* continued to stay hunkered down in the jungle foliage watching the pirates.

The messy weather had also kept Cooper and his friends from executing Como's plan. Today was going to be different though. With the pirates finishing the transfer of the goods, the chance to go forward with the plan had to take place today.

Thankfully, the weather seemed to be cooperating. It was still cloudy and the wind had picked up considerably, but at least the rain had stopped.

Cooper was glad that the rain had ended. He despised having his orange fur plastered to his body. Unfortunately, he now had to deal with the overwhelming fear of what Como had asked him to do.

The little spider monkey had come up with quite a plan to get Marisol's bird-shaped treasure back. Both Marisol and Marco thought it was a great idea, but Cooper wasn't so sure.

There were three parts to Como's plan or mission as he liked to call it. First, they had to get themselves onto the ship where young JJ Brooks was now living. Once they were on the *Adventure*, they had to figure out where JJ kept his personal items. Then they had to get back on the *Queen Anne's Revenge* hopefully without the pirates noticing.

Since the pirates anchored the ships close to each other, Como had originally planned to swing over to the *Adventure* by using the ropes in the sails and rigging. His plans changed when Blackbeard decided to put boards between the prize ship and the *Queen Anne's Revenge* to help transfer some of the cargo.

The pirates had also put boards between the *Queen Anne's Revenge* and the *Adventure* so they could move from ship to ship carrying armloads of goods. Como wanted to use them to get aboard the *Adventure*, too. This way, Cooper could help him look for the treasure.

All morning Cooper had been dreading this mission. He wanted to help get Marisol's treasure back, but walking across a board with the ocean below him was terrifying. To make matters worse, Como and the macaws had voted to keep the mission a secret from Tuffy.

Keeping the secret had been hard, especially since Tuffy had asked Cooper to help with the mouser duties numerous times. Today had started the same way with Cooper and Tuffy down in the ship's hold catching mice. The difference was, Cooper didn't stay down there. Instead, he waited until Tuffy started hunting before he returned to the main deck.

Cooper had just stepped out on the deck when he spotted Como. As soon as the little spider monkey saw him, he scampered over.

"Are you ready to go, Coop?" he asked.

"I guess."

"Did you take care of Tuffy? You know she wouldn't approve of us going over to the *Adventure*. She would only try to stop us."

"Tuffy is busy hunting," Cooper replied.

"Great! Let's go," Como exclaimed. "I have already let Marisol out of her cage. She's hiding up in the sails and will be our lookout in case we need to hurry back to the ship. We thought it was best for Marco to stay in his cage since his wing is still sore."

"What if Captain Blackbeard sees us?"

As if Cooper's words had summoned him, the fearsome pirate captain exited his cabin at the back of the ship. The red-bearded quartermaster, William Howard, was with him. Blackbeard appeared to be in an ornery mood.

Several members of the crew who were carrying supplies taken from the *Protestant Caesar* quickly moved out of his way. Only one man was brave enough to walk up to him. It was the cook, Joseph Curtice, otherwise known as Cookie.

"Captain, I thought ye should know that Stede just went over to the *Protestant Caesar*. Looked like he was carrying a logbook, a feathered quill, and an ink bottle," Cookie said.

Blackbeard sighed. "He's probably looking for someone to take him ashore. I told him we didn't have time to explore the land, but he's determined to sketch drawings of the unusual animals Honduras might have."

"Unusual animals my foot! He's lucky a wild beast hasn't eaten him during one of his explorations. Are ye sure he's even a pirate?"

"Bonnet believes he is. Anyway, I've got more important things to do than to concern myself with him."

"Maybe ye should tell Cookie, Thomas Miller, and Edward Salter what ye just told me," William suggested.

Two of the pirates heading down into the hold stopped in their tracks. Both men had been carrying small barrels on their shoulders. Edward was a bit shorter than Thomas. He was a cooper by trade, making barrels on land before taking a job on a merchant ship. When Blackbeard captured the ship Edward served on, he willingly joined the pirate crew. Thomas was an expert in navigation, which made him a valuable member of Blackbeard's crew as well.

"What's going on, Captain?" Thomas asked as he lifted his tricorn hat, pushed backed his dark hair, and wiped sweat from his brow.

"I just had a private meeting with William. He thinks I should share what we discussed."

"Ye can trust us, Captain," Thomas said.

"I know. Edward is loyal, ye might as well be third in command, and Cookie, well, we go way back," Blackbeard replied.

Cookie chuckled. "Aye. We've been friends for many years, long before we started our pirate careers two years ago. I know the real man behind that beard."

"There are a handful of us original crew left, Captain, and ye don't have to worry about where our loyalties are," William added.

"Thank ye. It isn't about loyalty exactly. I just know that some will question my decisions. As ye all know, I don't truly have control over the fleet. The rules state that pirate captains only have complete control during battle. At other times, each crew member gets to vote on major decisions," Blackbeard said.

"We can get the crew behind ye, if that's what ye need, Captain,"

Thomas offered.

"What is it ye are trying to do?" Cookie wanted to know.

"I don't want to kill Captain Wyer or the crew of the *Protestant Caesar*. My plan is to give Wyer a chance to surrender and to come aboard the *Queen* so I can question him. I know they have given us their ship, but they could have moved valuables to the jungle. After I interrogate them, I want to let them have their empty ship back. Also, I think we should release the crew of the *Land of Promise*. Most of them chose to remain prisoners. There is no need to keep them. It's just more mouths to feed," Blackbeard explained.

"I suggested to Captain that we go forward with his plan. If the crew questions him, then we will do whatever it takes to make sure it's a fair vote. Better to act now and seek others' opinions as a last resort, if ye ask me," William said.

"I agree," Cookie replied.

"Me too," Thomas added as Edward also nodded in agreement.

"It's settled then. Thomas, select a few of the crew to go with ye ashore. I want ye to personally talk to Captain Wyer. Tell him I wish to see him immediately, and make sure he understands it is in his best interest if he surrenders peacefully. Make it look good, if ye know what I mean," Blackbeard said.

Thomas grinned. "I know exactly what ye mean, Captain, and don't worry, he'll come."

"Good. In the meantime, Cookie, I want ye to keep a watchful eye on the men here on the *Queen*. William, ye will need to go over to the *Protestant Caesar* and be sure the men haven't overlooked anything valuable. I will be in my cabin preparing to meet with Wyer."

As the five pirates dispersed, Como grabbed fistfuls of Cooper's orange fur in his hands and started to shake him. "Do you know what this means, Coop? It means we can scoot right over to the *Adventure* without having to sneak over there. Blackbeard is so busy with his plan he won't even notice us!"

The little spider monkey let go of Cooper's fur and scampered over to the railing. Cooper reluctantly followed his friend. As he approached the railing, he could see the boards stretched across the short distance between the *Queen Anne's Revenge* and the *Adventure*. The wooden planks fit perfectly into the small slots at the bottom of the railing.

There were many slots on both sides of the ship which easily drained off any unwanted seawater or rainwater during storms. Even the deck was slightly higher in the center of the ship and slanted to each side so water could drain quickly.

Como jumped up to the top of the railing and disappeared on the other side. Seconds later, the little brown monkey was peeking under the hole and motioning for Cooper.

"What are you waiting for, Coop?" he asked.

Cooper felt sick. "Maybe we should rethink this, Como."

"Rethink it? This may be our only chance to retrieve Marisol's treasure for a very long time. You heard Blackbeard. He's planning to leave as soon as he talks to the captain of the *Protestant Caesar*."

"I'm not sure it's a chance we need to take."

"A chance is a funny thing, Coop. Sometimes you take a chance and it turns out good. Other times it turns out bad, but if you never take a chance at all, then what do you have?"

Cooper thought for a moment. "I don't know."

"Nothing. Which means we must at least try."

Taking a shaky breath, Cooper slowly nodded, knowing he wouldn't be able to change Como's mind. Trying to push away his fear, he jumped up to the top of the railing. He unsheathed his claws to get a better grip on the wooden surface.

As he looked down at the greenish-blue ocean below, a sickening feeling started to overwhelm him. Como was right beneath him wearing a big grin on his tan-colored face. With a flip of his long, flexible tail, the little monkey scampered across the plank with ease. Once he was safely on the other side, he grabbed the railing of the *Adventure* and swung himself up to it.

Now sitting on top of the railing, the little monkey again motioned for Cooper to follow. "You can do this, Coop. Just walk the plank like I did." Como suddenly started laughing. "Hey, that's funny! I've heard stories about pirates making their victims walk the plank."

"It isn't funny, it's terrifying," Cooper said.

"Come on, it is a *little* bit funny," Como replied as Cooper shook his head.

Crouching down so his belly fur brushed the wood, Cooper eased his front paws over the edge. In one sleek move, he gently came down on the wooden board. With his claws planted firmly into the wood, he slowly made some progress across the plank.

Then it happened. He didn't mean to look down, but his eyes drifted to the greenish-blue sea below him anyway. Small waves lapped against the hulls of both ships, making a slapping sound.

Fear engulfed Cooper's heart as he squatted in the middle of the plank unable to move. Thoughts of hungry sharks swirled in his mind. He was so scared his shaking body caused the board to sway up and down. Closing his eyes tight, he prayed for the Mighty Creator to help him.

"Don't stop now, Coop, you're almost here," Como encouraged him from the *Adventure*.

"I-I can't."

"Sure, you can. Take a deep breath and start crawling this way."

"Easy for you to say, you're used to climbing the sails and doing tricks up high. Besides, your tail is like another hand. It can grab things and helps you climb."

"Cats can climb too, Coop, and you have sharp claws and a tail that helps you keep your balance."

The little spider monkey had a point, even though Cooper didn't want to admit it. In his heart, he knew being a cat had nothing to do with the fear he just could not overcome.

Cooper opened one eye and then the other as he tried to gather himself. Keeping his claws firmly planted into the wood, he reached his front right paw out in front of him and cautiously eased forward. Slowly, Cooper inched his way across the remaining half of the plank.

At last, he made it to the other side. Como cheered for him as he let out a deep sigh of relief. Squatting on the plank, Cooper shook his tail and leapt up to the top of the *Adventure*'s railing beside Como.

"Way to go, Coop! I knew you could do it. Now, let's get going with our mission," the spider monkey said as he jumped down to the main deck.

In one leap, Cooper joined his friend. The *Adventure* looked more like the size of the *Revenge* than the enormous *Queen Anne's Revenge*. It had two masts instead of three and had a much smaller

quarterdeck above the captain's cabin.

Luckily, most of the crew was on the *Protestant Caesar*. Only a few pirates had stayed to keep everything in order on the *Adventure*. The ship's captain, Israel Hands, also seemed to be elsewhere.

"What are the two of you doing on my ship?" asked a voice.

Both Cooper and Como turned to see the young she-cat, Prissy, coming up from the stairs leading into the belly of the ship. The black cat trotted over to them and sat down, draping her long black tail around her body and across her white paws. She cocked her head to one side as she stared at them.

"We were just . . . exploring," Como muttered, giving Cooper a sideways look.

Cooper understood why Como was hesitant to tell Prissy about their mission, but he didn't think they had much of a choice. Prissy wasn't going to let them search *her* ship without an explanation.

"Let's tell her, Como. Maybe she can help us," Cooper suggested.

Como's dark brown eyes widened in surprise. "Are you sure?"

"I'm sitting right here, you know. Just spit it out. What can I do to help?" Prissy interrupted.

Glancing once more at Como, Cooper began to tell Prissy about Marisol and her treasure. He made sure to describe the bird-shaped flute in detail and mentioned how they had last seen it in the hands of the young pirate, JJ Brooks.

"I haven't seen anything like that onboard, but I can take you to the sailors' sleeping quarters. I remember the young pirate you are talking about, though I'm still learning who is who. Maybe he left this flute object near his hammock. Follow me," Prissy said.

With a flick of her tail, she headed for the stairway leading down into the ship. Cooper stayed close behind her as Como brought up the end. In no time the three of them were in the galley where a small fire burned in the coals beneath a large cauldron in the brick firepit. A single pirate was standing over the firepit dropping some sort of food into the black iron cauldron.

Thankfully, the pirate was too busy cooking to notice two cats and a monkey crossing the galley on their way to the sleeping quarters. Like other ships Cooper had served on, the sleeping quarters smelled musty from the mixture of salty sea air and sweat. Above them, rows of sailcloth hammocks hung from the wooden ceiling.

Prissy came to an abrupt stop about halfway down the corridor. She closed her eyes and sniffed the air in the direction of one of the hammocks. Cooper figured she must be trying to locate JJ's. Deciding to smell the air himself, Cooper took a deep breath.

It was difficult to pinpoint any specific human scent in all the mustiness already in the room, especially when Cooper hadn't been around JJ much to start with. Other than his own scent and Como's, all he could smell was the sweet scent he guessed belonged to Prissy.

"Well, I think this one is his. There isn't much to it, but you can look around," she said.

Como grabbed JJ's hammock in one hand and pulled himself up. While he inspected it from above, Cooper checked underneath the hammock. Unfortunately, there wasn't anything except the wooden floorboards.

"Looks like we're out of luck," Como sighed as he jumped down.

"I thought you didn't believe in luck," Cooper teased him.

Como smiled. "I believe in the good kind, not the bad kind that you seem to believe in."

"I don't want to believe in bad luck. It just seems to follow me."

"What are the two of you talking about?" Prissy interrupted.

Cooper glanced at Como, hoping the little monkey wouldn't tell Prissy about his bad luck streak.

"It doesn't matter. Is there anywhere else on this ship where JJ might have hidden the treasure?" Cooper asked Prissy.

"Not that I can think of," Prissy said. "I may not know these pirates well, but I know every nook and cranny of my ship. There are many places one could hide a treasure. I just don't recall seeing the young pirate anywhere other than his hammock, on deck, or with his father in the captain's cabin. We can check the cabin if you want."

"Let's go then," Como replied.

Prissy led the way back through the sleeping quarters toward the galley. She stopped in the doorway between the two rooms. Looking over her, Cooper could see the cook moving around the room with his mop and bucket. The pirate was humming a sea chantey tune as bubbling sounds came from the cauldron.

"We can't go through the galley, he'll see us. I don't know what those pirates might do to me if they find out I brought you down here. We will have to go out the other way. Follow me," Prissy said as she flicked her black tail and started trotting to the other end of the sleeping quarters.

"What does she mean?" Como whispered to Cooper. "I thought there was only one way out."

"I'm not sure, unless she's talking about the hatch at the front of the ship. I have seen sailors use it to load the ship to its full capacity. Come on," Cooper replied, running to catch up with Prissy.

By the time Cooper and Como had caught up with the young

she-cat, she was halfway down the steps which led to the bottom of the ship. Trying to keep up with her, Cooper quickly descended the stairs.

"Wait up, Coop," Como called out. "Look what I found."

Cooper stopped at the bottom of the stairs and turned to look up at his friend. The little spider monkey was holding up a gold coin.

"What are you going to do with it?" Cooper asked.

"Keep it, of course. It's shiny. I'm going to add it to my collection," he replied.

"You're as silly as Captain Bonnet is about collecting things."

"Collecting is fun," Como said, pausing for a moment. "Did you hear something down there, Coop?"

Even in the darkness, Cooper's green eyes noticed something odd about the way Como stared at him. He knew the noise probably came from the mice or rats who lived in the ship's hold, but it could have also been Prissy. Deciding to go with that possibility, he tried to reassure his friend.

"It was probably Prissy."

"I don't like it down here. I can't see well in the dark like you, Coop," Como said.

"Are you scared?" Cooper asked, shocked to hear the monkey admit to being afraid sometimes, too.

Como hesitated. "Maybe just a little."

"I understand how you feel, but we don't have a choice. Just stay close to me," Cooper replied.

The little spider monkey grabbed Cooper's orange tail. Holding it tightly in his furry hand, Como followed Cooper into the darkness. Having someone tugging on his tail felt uncomfortable, but

Cooper didn't complain. If it made Como feel better, then it was worth it.

As they went further into the darkness, Cooper sniffed the air for scents. Many smells came to him including the ship's chickens and those of the food and wine in the barrels. He could also smell the scent of freshly cut wood, though none was currently in the hold. Cooper remembered that the pirates left the log wood they discovered in the *Adventure*'s hold back on Turneffe Island to make room for any treasures they might obtain from other prize ships.

Among the other scents of cotton and sugar, Cooper tasted the horrible scent of the rats occupying the hold. Their foul scent caused Cooper to shiver. He despised those ugly, gray creatures.

Trying to block out their smell, Cooper attempted to locate Prissy by her sweet scent. Although it was too dark to see much ahead of them, he could tell they were getting closer to her. He also knew they should be nearing the middle of the ship where the ballast stones were located. Every ship had these stones in the hold.

Within moments, Cooper's paws brushed against a pile of rock-like objects. He quickly moved to the center of the room, knowing that the ballast stones would be on either side of the ship with only a narrow path in the center. This path lined up with the two great masts which came down through the decks above them. Ballast stones added weight to the center of the ships and kept them stabilized in the water, especially during storms.

At last, Cooper spotted Prissy's silhouette at the far end of the ship's bow where she appeared to be waiting for them. Cooper was about to tell Como, when something suddenly came out from the nearest pile of ballast stones.

Como squealed in surprise as he jumped up on top of Cooper's back as if he were riding him. Startled, Cooper collapsed to the deck under the monkey's weight. He looked wildly around him, scenting the air as a hissing sound grabbed Cooper's attention. His green eyes instantly recognized the small, dark gray beast. It was a rat!

Shaking Como off his back, Cooper got between his friend and the rat. He unsheathed his claws, arched his back, and let out a hiss of his own, hoping to scare off the gray beast. His mind whirred as he wondered what he was going to do next. Rats were vicious beasts that not only fought hard, but also had quite a nasty bite.

Cooper couldn't help but remember all his bad encounters with rats over his short career as a ship's cat. Each one had turned out badly as fear always seemed to get the best of Cooper.

Apparently seeing what was happening, Prissy came back to help. She bravely stood beside Cooper, aching her back and hissing in the rat's direction. With both cats showing their teeth, the rat must have thought twice about attacking because it quickly turned and ran off.

Prissy announced that she would come back to kill the rat later, though she admitted it would be a tough battle. The black and white she-cat didn't linger as she hurried back to the front of the ship. Relieved, Cooper let out a deep breath and tried to relax his fur while he and Como ran to catch up with her.

By the time the two friends came to a stop beside her, Prissy was climbing a wooden ladder that went up to the second level. Cooper knew from his experience on the *La Concorde* that another short ladder connected the second level to the top deck. This enabled the sailors to easily fill the hold from above.

Not wanting to spend another moment in the ship's hold, Cooper unsheathed his claws and grabbed the first rung of the ladder. Digging his claws deep into the wood, he stretched his body upward to grab the next rung. Como followed close behind, obviously not wanting to stay in the darkness any more than Cooper did.

In no time, the three of them had made it to the second level and were climbing up the last ladder to the top. Cooper purred in happiness as he felt the warmth on his fur and tasted the salty sea air.

Once they were near the top deck, Prissy cautiously peered out of the hatch to check things out. She quickly reported no pirates were near enough to see them coming up from the hold. Cooper followed Prissy out onto the main deck with Como behind him, glad that no one spotted them.

Prissy led them to the rear or stern of the ship, staying close to the *Adventure*'s railing. When they were almost at the captain's cabin, a loud shriek echoed from the sails and rigging above them. Looking up, Cooper recognized Marisol's red and blue feathers as she soared through the air.

"Hurry! Hurry!" the macaw squawked.

"What's going on?" Cooper yelled back.

Marisol landed on the deck beside them. "I've been trying to warn you for a while now, but I couldn't see either of you on deck. Captain Blackbeard finished his meeting with Captain Wyer and sent him back to land. Blackbeard told the pirates he decided to release Captain Wyer and his men. He also ordered the crew to burn the *Protestant Caesar*."

"Burn it? Why aren't they going to keep it like they did my ship and the others?" Prissy asked.

The scarlet macaw cocked her head to one side. "Who is this cat?"

"Marisol, this is Prissy. She's the ship's cat for the *Adventure*, and Prissy, this is our friend we told you about," Cooper explained as the two of them said hello to each other. "So, what's this about burning the ship?"

"I don't understand his reason, and it doesn't matter. The most important thing is Blackbeard's other command. He told his men to remove the planks between the ships. If you don't hurry, you won't be able to get back onto the *Queen Anne's Revenge*," Marisol told them.

Como gasped. "Let's go!"

"What are we going to do about Marisol's treasure? We were going to check the captain's cabin," Cooper pointed out.

"I can continue to look for it," Prissy offered.

"Thank you," Marisol replied as she flapped her wings excitedly.

"Come on, Coop. We better hurry back to the *Queen Anne's Revenge*," Como said. "See you later, Prissy."

Holding tightly to his gold coin, the little spider monkey scampered over to the railing where the wooden plank fit into one of the water slots. He jumped up on top of the railing and without hesitation disappeared on the other side. Meanwhile, Marisol said goodbye to Prissy before taking flight. She soared through ropes and sails to the adjoining ship, leaving Cooper alone with the she-cat.

Feeling a bit awkward, Cooper glanced at the black and white she-cat unsure of what he should say. Knowing he didn't have much time, he quickly thanked her for all her help and said a simple goodbye before unsheathing his claws and jumping on top of the ship's railing.

"Goodbye to you, Cooper, and good luck," Prissy replied.

Dipping his head in acknowledgment, Cooper carefully balanced himself on the plank below him. He tried to keep his focus on the ship ahead instead of the churning sea, but his nerves still made his stomach feel queasy.

Unlike before, Como didn't wait for him to cross the plank. At first Cooper thought this was odd, but he was too concerned about falling into the greenish-blue water to dwell on it. He had to concentrate to keep his paws on the wooden plank and even the slightest mistake could be deadly.

Cooper was almost close enough to jump up on the railing of the *Queen Anne's Revenge* when the plank suddenly moved beneath him. To his horror, he realized someone was pulling the plank through the slot and onto the ship.

A quick look at the *Adventure* behind him told Cooper he didn't have much time to react. Fear gripped his heart and his mind whirled as he debated what to do.

His green eyes spotted Marisol flying high into the rigging. She then dropped out of the sky and plummeted to the deck of the *Queen Anne's Revenge.*

"My goodness! That's my scarlet macaw," Stede Bonnet's voice shouted from the other side of the ship's railing.

Although Cooper couldn't see the so-called captain, there was no mistaking who it was. He waited to hear if Marisol was okay, but another jerk of the plank nearly caused Cooper to lose his balance.

Cooper clung to the plank with all his might, feeling the wood threaten to rip his claws out of his paws. He looked wildly around for options while simultaneously begging the Mighty Creator for help.

A third lurch of the wooden plank dislodged it from the *Adventure*,

forcing Cooper to claw his way up the plank to keep from falling into the sea. Using his back legs, he lunged upward, barely grabbing the railing with his front claws as the plank disappeared from the slot.

Holding onto the railing proved to be almost impossible. His back paws hung in the air, attempting to locate anything solid. Exhausted, Cooper finally managed to get his back legs high enough so he could get his back claws into the wooden railing.

With his back paws in a better position, he summoned all his remaining strength and reached out to pull himself up to the top of the railing. Cooper peeped over the top just as a pirate stood up. The sudden movement scared Cooper so much he nearly lost his grip. To make things worse, the pirate staring back at him was none other than Captain Blackbeard.

"How did ye get out there?" asked the tall, bearded captain.

The pirate captain roughly grabbed Cooper by the scruff of his neck and held him up. Feeling relieved to be safe on the ship, Cooper couldn't help but also feel fearful of what the pirate would do. It was obvious the captain was not pleased to see him.

Blackbeard's dark brown eyes penetrated Cooper's green ones as if he was trying to understand his thoughts. Cooper bravely stared back at him, not wanting to show fear or the pain he was experiencing from the tight grip of Blackbeard's fingers digging into the fur at the back of his shoulders.

A noisy fuss pulled Blackbeard's attention away from Cooper to something on his leg. The pirate captain shook his left leg as he angrily cursed. Cooper soon realized it was the little spider monkey.

"Ye don't have to kick my monkey," Stede Bonnet said as he stepped up to Blackbeard holding Marisol in his arms.

"If ye don't do something with these animals I will lock them in the hold. I'm not going to put up with that monkey attacking me. Do ye understand?" Blackbeard snapped.

Stede stooped to grab Como from the deck. His demeanor had changed and it was clear he feared the notorious pirate.

"I don't know what has gotten into them," Stede mumbled. "It's strange how this macaw got out of her cage, and how she acted as if she had fallen out of the sky. I can't see anything wrong with her."

"Just remember what I said, Stede," Blackbeard warned.

The pirate captain placed Cooper on the deck by his black boots. Cooper gazed up into his bearded face, grateful the pirate released him instead of punishing him.

Then, to his surprise, Cooper caught a glimpse of a brief smile on the pirate's wind-chapped lips as the captain ran his rough hand across Cooper's forehead and down his back. Confused by his smile, Cooper realized he had just witnessed a rare peek into the man beneath the beard so many souls feared to cross.

CHAPTER FIVE

Horizons

Each new day brought the same series of events as the day before. From the time the first rays of the sun peeked over the eastern horizon until the bright red ball disappeared into the ocean in the west, the pirates worked and sweated. The predictable days brought some comfort to Cooper, who was glad to finally be back out on the open sea sailing instead of committing piracy.

Regardless of whether the crew were pirates, they still had the same work as any other sailor. Ropes and sails had constant adjusting, sailcloth needed mending, and the deck required caulking and water-proofing with oakum. Luckily, the pirates had found plenty of barrels of oakum on one of the ships they captured at Turneffe Island.

On the days when the pirates were stuffing the seams in between the boards with oakum, Cooper and Como stayed inside the captain's cabin with Marisol and Marco. Cooper despised the nasty smell of the oakum, which was a mixture of hemp fibers like those made into ropes and tar from pine trees.

The worst part about caulking the seams was how sticky it made the deck until it had time to dry and harden. It was a messy process that started with the pirates removing old oakum and replacing rotten

boards. Next, Cookie heated up the oakum in a large cauldron used only for this job. Once hot, the pirates pounded the oakum into the cracks with iron tools.

Cooper had overheard Captain Blackbeard telling Cookie he planned to have the crew check the outside hull of the *Queen Anne's Revenge* for any needed repairs when they arrived at Nassau. He also wanted them to repair the other five ships in the fleet while they anchored at the island.

News of Captain Blackbeard's plans to go to Nassau intrigued Cooper. He had never been there, but from what Tuffy had told him, it was a grand island. Unlike Turneffe Island, Nassau was large enough for humans to have a sort of town there.

At one time, the Queen of England controlled Nassau, but when she died things changed. Pirates didn't approve of the new king who took the queen's place. According to Tuffy, pirates had slowly taken over the island. Now it was a perfect place for pirates to hide out.

Thinking about Nassau made Cooper wonder what things would be like once they arrived. It was hard to imagine an island full of pirates. As Cooper pondered all this, he decided to give his orange fur coat a good licking. A ship's cat had to at least keep his appearance looking decent.

Cooper sat on a straight-backed chair in the corner of the captain's cabin licking his fur. The steady rhythm of his tongue against his fur soothed his nerves. Earlier, Como had asked if he wanted to go out on the deck to play, but Tuffy insisted he needed to practice his hunting moves.

Her determination to teach Cooper how to fight rats drove him crazy. The last thing he wanted to do was fight the rats. Unfortunately,

Tuffy wouldn't accept this. She was certain that a ship cat's duty was to protect the ship from *all* rodents, not just the mice, and until Cooper learned to deal with them, she was going to keep training him. Today's lesson had been in the captain's cabin.

Once Cooper had groomed his back and chest fur, he licked his right paw and swiped it over his ear to clean his face. He switched paws to clean his other ear when his eyes caught a glimpse of black up on the captain's desk.

Tuffy, who had been grooming her fur in one of the two chairs positioned in front of the desk, had just jumped up on top of it. The solid black cat pranced across the strewn papers and maps attempting to grab her captain's attention.

Blackbeard sat at his desk writing in a black, leather-bound book. He continuously paused to dip his turkey feather quill into the small inkwell sitting on his desk. Cooper had noticed the pirate captain writing in this logbook nearly every night and occasionally during the daylight hours as he was doing today. Whatever he wrote in it must be important because Blackbeard always locked it in the bottom drawer of his desk.

Sighing, Captain Blackbeard put down the turkey feather quill as he rubbed Tuffy's black fur. "What are ye trying to tell me, girl? Is bad weather coming? Nay, I don't think that's it. Perhaps ye are only reminding me to check on my men. We should be nearing New Providence by now."

Tuffy flicked her black tail from side to side and let out a purr. Suddenly, the door to the cabin opened and in walked the boatswain, Garret Gibbons. His job was to oversee any repairs of the sails and to keep the crew busy moving the ropes and sails to catch the wind.

"Captain, land is in sight. I sent Nathaniel Jackson up in the rigging with a spyglass to see how many other ships are in the cove."

"Good thinking. I'll be out there shortly," Blackbeard replied.

Garret nodded in understanding as he exited the quarters. Meanwhile, Blackbeard slid his logbook back into the bottom drawer and locked it. As he stood up, he paused to scratch Tuffy behind her ears and under her chin.

"Alright, Tuffy, it's time for us to do our duty. Let's get out on deck. Ye know how those scoundrels are. Some of them wouldn't make it without my instructions," Blackbeard said with a chuckle.

The pirate captain lifted Tuffy off his desk and placed her on the wooden floorboards. He then grabbed his tricorn hat and put it on his head as he made his way to the door. Tuffy followed behind him, holding her head high and her tail straight. She stopped at Blackbeard's boots as he opened the door and motioned for her to go first. Instead, Tuffy turned to Cooper.

"Come along, Cooper. Captain needs our help," she told him.

Obviously, Blackbeard couldn't understand what the she-cat was saying, but her meows made him laugh.

"I forgot ye were over there, Cooper. Guess Tuffy has sort of adopted ye as her own. She's old enough to be ye mother. Well, let's get going then. The crew is waiting for us," he said.

Cooper jumped down from the straight-backed chair and hurried over to the open door. He followed Tuffy outside as Captain Blackbeard closed the door behind them.

The bright sun was low in the western horizon showing how late in the day it was. This didn't seem to bother the pirates. They were so busy pulling ropes and moving sails none of them even stopped when their captain appeared on deck with the two ship's cats.

Captain Blackbeard walked to the center of the deck where his quartermaster, William Howard, talked with the third ranked pirate, Thomas Miller. The two men were communicating with Nathaniel Jackson who was still up in the rigging holding on to the main mast.

"Follow me, Cooper, we have work to do," Tuffy said as she made her way to the ship's railing.

Wondering what she meant, Cooper obediently trotted after her. The two of them walked swiftly toward the front of the ship, staying close to the railing. Cooper noticed how Tuffy slowed her pace three times. Each time she sniffed the air before she picked up her pace again.

Soon they reached the bow of the ship. Tuffy stopped abruptly at the very peak. She jumped up on the flat board that reinforced the tip of the ship and motioned with a flick of her long, black tail for Cooper to join her. With a shake of his haunches, Cooper leapt up beside her.

"What do you see, Cooper?" she asked.

Cooper stared at the horizon. He could see a large mass of land up ahead and the big sky doused in hues of red and yellow. There were also seabirds flying in the air and of course the greenish-blue ocean below them that was steadily growing greener as the ship went over the coral reefs and shallow sandbars under the water.

Not sure what Tuffy was expecting him to say, Cooper told her all the things he could see. She then asked him what he smelled. Thinking this was odd, Cooper began with the most obvious scent of the salty sea air.

To his surprise, the more he sniffed the air, the more scents he noticed. There was the fresh oakum between the boards, the smell of sweat no doubt from the pirates, a slight smell coming from the chickens, Tuffy's own scent, and that of something far away, yet somehow carried by the wind. It took a moment or two for Cooper to figure out what it was, but he soon realized it was the smell of dirt; a clear sign of the land ahead.

"I can see you're surprised by what you smell," Tuffy said. "I'm guessing this is the first time you really studied your surroundings. Remember this, Cooper, and you will become a reliable ship's cat."

The one-eyed, black cat started to jump down, but Cooper stopped her. "I don't understand. What does this have to do with being a mouser? I thought our duty was to keep the mice and rats from eating the food supply or damaging the ship's hull."

"Yes, those are the duties of a mouser, but being a ship's cat is much more, or at least it should be. Many cats will get a chance to be a mouser of a ship. Humans need us. They depend on our skills. The problem is, most ship's cats think their duties are only below deck. We have a higher calling though. A true ship's cat will have other valuable qualities."

"Like what?" Cooper asked.

"Well, for instance, what I just told you about noticing your surroundings. Humans can't smell as well as we can so it's our duty to alert the captain if we smell something unusual or dangerous."

"I didn't smell anything strange other than dirt, and Captain Blackbeard already knows we're near land," Cooper pointed out.

Tuffy smiled. "I know, I smelled it, too. If there had been something to worry about, I would have made you focus on the scent until you discovered it. The crew saw the land this time, but next time it might be something else. Sometimes I can smell rain coming or feel it in my bones. Captain depends on me to tell him of such things. It's also my duty to keep an eye on the crew, and to warn him if I sense an uprising."

"I thought the quartermaster was supposed to watch them."

"He does, but sometimes the men are alone together. With so many outsiders forced into piracy or even choosing to become pirates, you can never tell if they will change their minds and attempt to take over. Captain and his loyal friends can't be everywhere so I help them. I make my daily rounds, listening to their scuttlebutt."

"Scuttlebutt?"

"Yes, that is what sailors nicknamed the barrel they drink water from. It also means gossip, which is what we'll be listening for."

"I don't think they would like it very much if I started hanging around," Cooper said.

"Why not? You are a ship's cat, aren't you?"

"I'm a bad omen, at least that's what the crew of the *Revenge* thinks. They would yell and try to kick me, but I always jumped out of their way. The other ships in this pirate fleet treated me the same. Captain Bonnet is the only one who doesn't think I'm a bad omen."

"I've told you what I thought about this silly bad omen talk. Now, what about your previous captain, you know, the one Captain Blackbeard stole this ship from. Did he choose you to be his ship's cat?"

Cooper looked down at his orange paws in shame. He didn't want to tell Tuffy the truth, but she seemed to have already guessed it.

"No, he got stuck with me. I was born in France a little over a year ago. Humans took me to the shipyard as soon as I was old enough to leave my mother. At first it wasn't so bad because I was with my siblings, but we soon found out the humans planned to sell us to sea captains. By the time Captain Pierre Dosset came, all my siblings had new homes except for me and one of my sisters. She had been small since birth and was still a bit wobbly on her legs so Captain Dosset chose me. I knew from the start he didn't like me, but he had no other choice. Later, I found out his previous mouser had gotten sick the day before and was unfit to travel. We left France the same day," Cooper told her.

"That explains a lot. Sounds like you didn't get any training. Of course, I'm not talking about formal training from the humans. I mean the kind of training young cats get from their mothers who are also mousers or from other experienced ship's cats. Don't worry, I will teach you as much as I can. Now, come on, we need to check the other side of the ship."

The black she-cat jumped to the deck and started down the other side of the ship, staying close to the railing as she had done before. Cooper followed close behind, bewildered by her words and determined to learn all he could from her.

By the time they reached the stern of the ship, Cooper noticed Captain Stede Bonnet was now on the quarterdeck with Captain Blackbeard. Bonnet must have been expecting to go ashore soon because he had changed into his fancy coat with its shiny gold buttons and was now wearing his feathered three-cornered hat instead of his work one.

"Hello, Coop!" called Como's unmistakable voice.

Cooper looked up into the rigging just in time to see the little spider monkey grab a rope with his long tail and swing to a rope tied to the mainsail. With one swift movement, he let go and slid down the sail cloth. When he was at the bottom, he gracefully dropped down to the wooden deck landing with a thud on his feet.

"Did you hear the news? We will be anchoring at Nassau soon," the little monkey said.

"Yes, we heard," Cooper replied. Then to Tuffy he added, "Why did Captain Blackbeard call the island New Providence instead of Nassau?"

"There is a chain of islands called the Bahamas. Originally, sailors named one of the islands Providence, after the old Providence. Years later there was some confusion over the names. Sailors started adding 'New' to the name to keep them apart. Eventually, the population on the island grew enough to call the tiny town Nassau. Although it is still small, it has become a much fought-over location. The English have tried numerous times to keep a government control, but so far none have succeeded. Pirates currently control it, or at least they did the last time we were there," Tuffy explained.

Before long, *Queen Anne's Revenge* and the fleet of ships behind her were entering the bay of New Providence Island. Cooper and Como watched from the stairs leading up to the quarterdeck. Below them, the pirates prepared to let down the anchor.

Once the ship was near the island, Captain Blackbeard commanded the men to release the iron chains. Seconds later, the heavy chains fell into the water with a splash. Similar sounds echoed nearby as the other four ships started dropping their anchors as well.

Then came the whirlwind of chaos as the pirates tied off ropes and uncovered the periauger boat in the center of the ship. Tuffy bravely made her way through their hurried feet, but Cooper stayed beside Como. He certainly didn't want to make the pirates mad by getting in their way.

In no time, the pirates had lifted the periauger off the deck and had it over the side of the ship. Using ropes and an iron pulley system, they lowered it into the water and let down the rope ladder. With the boat ready, Captain Blackbeard chose who would go ashore first.

One by one, the handful of chosen pirates climbed down the rope ladder. Blackbeard was the last to join them after he had given the quartermaster, William Howard, some instructions. Stede Bonnet tried to get Blackbeard to let him go ashore too, but the bearded captain outsmarted him by saying he was now in charge of the *Queen Anne's Revenge.* Cooper saw Blackbeard give William a wink, which no doubt meant he was leaving the ship in his hands instead of Stede's.

The tall, bearded captain then swung his right leg over the ship's railing and disappeared down the rope ladder. After a few minutes had passed, Cooper could see the periauger moving away from the *Queen Anne's Revenge.* All six of the chosen crew members were swiftly rowing the small boat toward land while Blackbeard sat at the rear surveying the island with his spyglass.

Knowing it could be a while before the pirates returned, Cooper crouched down and tucked his paws under him as Como started talking about what the island might be like and shared his hope that there weren't any crocodillies. At some point, the little spider monkey changed topics. Cooper listened to his friend describe the island he came from and the stories of his spider monkey tribe.

Time passed, and soon the sky was a deep purple. Only a small amount of red remained in the sky where the sun had once been. Stars had started to make their grand appearance, but the moon was absent from the night's sky. A couple of pirates began to light the candles in the iron lanterns when someone gave a shout.

Cooper recognized the young man up in the rigging as Nathaniel Jackson, one of the ship's lookouts. The pirate announced the periauger was back. Hearing the news, William Howard called all the men to come help haul it up.

Although it was dark without the moon, the light emitting from the lanterns aided the pirates as they dropped down some ropes so their comrades could tie them to the periauger. Cookie threw the rope ladder over the side and the men in the boat started to climb up on deck.

"Come on, Coop, let's get closer," Como said as he hopped up and went down to the deck.

Following his furry friend, Cooper made his way down the stairs. By the time they were in front of the captain's cabin, Tuffy was trotting swiftly over to them.

"There you are," she said as she came to a stop in front of the cabin. "I was wondering where the two of you were. Captain will most likely be giving everyone an update."

The pirates began to heave the ropes over the pulleys until they hauled up the periauger. Once they had it back in the center of the ship, Captain Blackbeard called a meeting.

"Listen up, men," Blackbeard yelled. "Nassau is full of pirates, both friends and perhaps a few enemies. We will stay here tonight and will go ashore tomorrow. That's all, return to ye posts."

"Who is there?" one of the pirates asked.

Even in the dim light, Cooper could see that Blackbeard wasn't too happy with the pirate's question. Cookie must have sensed it too because he quickly interrupted.

"Come along, fellows, my cauldron of stew should be ready to eat," he said hastily.

The cook glanced at his captain before heading down into the galley. A stream of the pirates joined him. While they went to get a bite to eat, Thomas Miller, Garret Gibbons, and William Howard approached their captain. Stede Bonnet came up to him as well, though he was a bit skittish.

"What are we facing, Captain? How many of our enemies are on the island?" William asked quietly.

"Just a few, if I had to guess. Most of them are friends. Charles Vane is here and so is Paulsgrave Williams," Blackbeard replied.

Garret glanced at the others. "Vane, huh? That'll be interesting. Ye know his quartermaster, Calico Jack Rackham, is with him. Calico is always up to something."

"Ye can bet on it," Thomas added. "Didn't Williams sail with 'Black' Sam Bellamy?"

Blackbeard nodded. "Aye. He took over for him after Sam's ship wrecked off Baltimore, Maryland. Sam was a good man and a friend of mine. If he trusted Paulsgrave then I certainly do."

The men nodded and slowly dispersed while their captain went into his cabin. As they were leaving, Tuffy let out a sigh.

"What's wrong?" Cooper asked her.

"Captain said there are a few enemies on the island. That means we will have to be extra cautious. He didn't say much about Captain Vane and Calico Jack, but I remember how wild and crazy their crew is. Luckily, Calico will be easy to keep an eye on since he always wears a colorful patchwork coat. His real name is John Rackham, but everyone calls him Calico Jack. Guess they thought he looked like a calico cat in his coat."

"Why do we need to be cautious?" Como wanted to know.

"Because the pirates aren't the only wild ones. Most ships have a ship's cat and pirate ships are no exception. Pirate cats can be just as crazy and dangerous as their captains or crew. I have met many of these cats and believe me, you don't want to cross them. Get some rest. We don't know what may be on our horizons."

Cooper and Como exchanged a worried look as the she-cat's words sunk in. He recalled Captain Blackbeard's plan to check and repair the bottoms of the ships when they reached the island. This meant the pirates would possibly take them off the ship until they could finish the repairs. Suddenly, Cooper felt anxious. It sounded as though they might come face to face with these rogue ship cats.

 CHAPTER SIX 

Captains' Toast

Flickers of sunlight nearly blinded Cooper as he hunkered down beside Como and Tuffy in their wooden cage. Captain Stede Bonnet sat behind them wearing his fancy attire. He hummed a sea chantey while the other four pirates rowed the periauger toward New Providence Island.

As the pirates dipped the oars in and out of the green seawater, the setting sun appeared and disappeared over the side of the small boat. Between the rocking and his nerves, Cooper felt sick. Part of him was fearful about this new adventure while the other part was surprisingly a bit excited.

For the last few days, the pirates had been working hard. Captain Blackbeard had ordered his men to remove some of the heavier supplies off the five ships. The plan was to pull the ships one by one on their sides so the pirates could check the outside of the hulls for any damage.

Prissy's ship, the *Adventure*, had been the first ship repaired. Since it didn't need any major replacements, Captain Blackbeard had ordered half the men to start working on the *Queen Anne's Revenge*. He also announced that tonight the crews would be going ashore. Only a handful of pirates were supposed to stay behind to guard the ships.

With most of the pirates going to Nassau to meet up with old comrades, Captain Stede Bonnet insisted his exotic creatures go ashore with him. He also scooped up Cooper and Tuffy, saying they would only get in the way of the next day's work so they might as well go along.

Cooper was glad to be with his friends even if he didn't know what to expect with the new adventure. At least they had each other. The pirates had taken Prissy to the island earlier in the day. Como had watched the crew of the *Adventure* put Prissy into a cage and load her into their periauger.

Thinking about Prissy made Cooper wonder if she had any luck finding Marisol's treasure. It had been over a half a moon since he and Como were on the *Adventure*. Surely, she had seen the clay flute by now. If nothing else, maybe she had new information about it.

From Cooper's point of view in the bottom of the periauger, it appeared like the pirates were nearing a small dock. In no time, they were tying ropes to the posts to hold the periauger still.

Captain Stede Bonnet was the first to climb out of the boat, followed by John Philips and Owen Roberts. Richard Greensail and James White stayed in the boat. The two dark-skinned men lifted Marisol and Marco's cage up onto the dock and slid it to their crew-mates. Next, they lifted the cage holding Cooper, Como, and Tuffy.

Unsheathing his claws, Cooper held on for dear life. As the pirates lifted them from the periauger, he could see the last red rays of sunlight in the horizon. The setting sun made the buttons on Stede's gray coat shine even brighter.

Recalling Tuffy's advice on how to be a ship's cat, Cooper sniffed the air. He immediately tasted the salt in the air and a variety of land-related smells. There was something else though, something he couldn't quite figure out. It wasn't exactly a smell. In fact, it was more like a feeling.

Just as Cooper was realizing this, the prickle went down his spine. The feeling made his orange fur stand up. Although Cooper couldn't remember ever feeling this way, he somehow knew it was some sort of warning.

"You feel it, don't you, Cooper?" Tuffy asked, evidently noticing how tense he had become.

Cooper nodded. "I feel something. What is it? Am I going crazy?"

"No, your instincts are kicking in. I feel it, too," she said.

"I don't feel anything," Como added.

Tuffy let out a purr of laughter. "I doubt you will. As far as I know, monkeys don't get these warnings. It's what makes us a good ship's cat. I have had these feelings for years. Each time I have one, something dangerous happens like a storm or a battle."

"There aren't any rain clouds. It looks like it will be a clear night," Como pointed out.

"We still need to be cautious," Tuffy reminded them.

Two of the pirates picked up Marco and Marisol's cage and carried them down the wooden dock toward the shore. The macaws squawked loudly while Captain Stede Bonnet begged the pirates to be careful with his special creatures.

When the pirates returned, they picked up the cage Cooper, Como, and Tuffy were in. Gripping the wood with his claws, Cooper watched the periauger grow smaller as the two pirates carried them down the wooden dock.

Captain Stede Bonnet walked behind them, adjusting his feathered, tricorn hat and dusting off the front of his gray coat. Cooper sensed that the gentleman pirate was nervous too, though he couldn't understand why.

Soon, the pirates were stepping off the wooden dock. John Philips and Owen Roberts carried the cage to a pile of other goods waiting on the sandy shore. The huge pile consisted of barrels, crates, and ballast stones moved from the ships.

A few pirates stood guard over the goods, no doubt to keep other pirate crews from stealing the supplies. Cooper recognized the three men from the day he and Como went looking for Marisol's treasure on Prissy's ship. They were members of the *Adventure*'s crew.

John and Owen put the cage holding Cooper, Como, and Tuffy on the ground beside Marisol and Marco's cage. Prissy was sitting in a cage of her own, watching them as she purred.

"It sure is good to see all of you!" she exclaimed.

"Who are you?" Marco asked, cocking his blue head to one side.

"That's Prissy, the cat we told you about," Marisol said. Then to Prissy she added, "Have you had any luck finding my treasure?"

"I have seen it twice, but the young pirate, JJ, always keeps it on him. So far, I haven't been able to get it," Prissy replied.

"What are you talking about? I haven't heard anything about any treasures," Tuffy interrupted.

Como and Cooper exchanged an uneasy look. The secret they had been trying to keep from Tuffy was now out in the open. There was no choice but to fill her in on everything.

Starting from the beginning, Cooper and Como told Tuffy about

Marisol's ocarina flute. Occasionally, the macaws would add details to the story and Prissy even made a few comments when they got to the part about searching her ship. Tuffy sat quietly, listening to the whole thing. When they finished, Tuffy spoke up.

"I see. Well, I guess we need a plan. Any suggestions?"

"A plan? Does that mean you are going to help us get it back?" Como asked in surprise.

"Why wouldn't I help? I'm a pirate cat, you know. Pirates are always up for a little adventure," she said as she winked her single eye.

"I don't see how we can have any sort of adventure while we're locked up in here. Looks like we won't get a chance to find Marisol's treasure now," Marco pointed out.

"I have an idea, but we will have to make sure the pirates don't see us," Prissy said as she began to share her idea with the group.

Everyone agreed to try it as soon as it was dark. With the sun already gone from the sky, it didn't take long for the stars to replace the streaks of red and orange clouds. While the friends waited, they listened to Captain Bonnet's nearly constant chatter.

The three pirates who were guarding the goods were clearly growing tired of Bonnet, but they didn't try to run him off. They stood guard as their fellow crewmates continued to make trips from the five ships to the dock, bringing boatloads of pirates with them each time.

Soon it was too dark to see how many pirates were on the shore. Several of them lit a few lanterns, but it was still impossible to count all the faces in the shadows. There was one face Cooper recognized. It was none other than Captain Blackbeard.

The tall, bearded captain put two fingers in his mouth and let out a whistle. Once he had the pirates' attention, Blackbeard told them they could enjoy themselves, but they better not stir up any trouble with other pirate crews. His tone of voice was serious, as if he had experienced similar bad behavior from his crew in the past.

When he finished, the entire group headed toward a glowing area further up the beach. Cooper guessed that the light was coming from the town Tuffy had told him about.

In no time, only three pirates remained to guard the supplies. It didn't take long for the sailors to pull out a bottle of spirits and begin passing it around.

While they swapped sips and seaside stories, Como set to work on the mission to escape. Reaching his little furry hand between the wooden bars of the cage, Como tried to grab the latch on Prissy's cage. Although the cages were sitting beside each other, Como still couldn't quite touch the handle of the latch.

Frustrated, Como sank down in the bottom of the cage and shook his head. "It's no use. I can't reach it. What are we going to do now?"

"Try to reach it with your tail," Cooper suggested. "It's longer than your arm and can grip things the same way."

Como grinned. "You are brilliant, Coop!"

The spider monkey stuck his long tail between the bars of the cage. With his backside close to the bars, he was able to reach the latch. Since Como couldn't see behind him, Cooper had to coach him on which way to flip his tail, but eventually the little monkey managed to grab it.

After a few jerks of his tail, Como succeeded in sliding the latch open. Prissy immediately nudged the door with her muzzle and stepped out. Acting quickly, the black and white she-cat used her muzzle and forehead to slide open the latch on Cooper, Como, and Tuffy's cage.

Relieved to be free, Cooper left the cramped cage. He arched his back and stretched his claws out in front of him while Como hurriedly freed Marisol and Marco. Once the macaws were ready to go, the six friends cautiously made their way around some barrels and away from the three pirates.

They were almost in the clear when Cooper heard the same sound he noticed before. Listening intently, he realized it was someone other than the pirates talking.

"Wait!" the voice hissed into the darkness.

Cooper stopped in his tracks. "Did you hear that?"

He looked around, trying to figure out where the voice came from. His friends walked back to him as the voice spoke again.

"Come over here. We need some help."

Without a word, Tuffy walked in the direction of the voice. Everyone followed her and to their surprise they discovered three cages with a cat in each of them.

"Hello, I'm Tuffy, one of the ship's cats of the *Queen Anne's Revenge*. Who are you? Do you belong to a ship in Captain Blackbeard's fleet?" Tuffy asked the three cats.

"We don't exactly belong, but I guess we are part of it anyway. Blackbeard captured our ships at Turneffe Island. I'm Blaze, the ship's cat for the *Adventure II*," the dark gray tabby said.

A gray cat spoke next. "My name is Gunner. The ship I served on was the one those pirates decided to burn. Blackbeard moved me to the *Revenge*."

The last cat dipped his head down as if he were showing Tuffy respect. His black fur was so long and thick it was difficult to see his yellow eyes. Cooper noticed he had some patches of gray in his fur too, a sign of his apparent age.

"And I am the honorable Sir Whiskers. My faithful crew had a terrible misfortune. Not only did those despicable pirates take our grand ship, but they ended up stranding most of our crew in Honduras. Our ship is a splendid—"

"Would you please drop the fancy words?" Blaze interrupted him in a clearly annoyed tone. Then to Tuffy he added, "He's the ship's cat for the *Land of Promise*."

"It's nice to meet all of you," Prissy replied. "I'm Prissy, the ship's cat for the *Adventure* and this is Cooper, the other ship's cat for the *Queen Anne's Revenge*. The spider monkey is Como and the macaws are Marisol and Marco."

"Now that we know each other, let's do something about getting you out of those cages," Tuffy offered.

The one-eyed, black cat nudged the latch on Gunner's cage while Prissy worked on Blaze's cage and Como opened the one holding Sir Whiskers. Once they were all free, Tuffy explained their mission to find Marisol's treasure. Then the group slipped away from the beach with Tuffy and Sir Whiskers in the lead and the macaws flying overhead as lookouts.

Cooper fell in line with Como, watching Blaze and Prissy who were walking in front of them. The little spider monkey was talking about the glowing lanterns in the distance, but Cooper wasn't listening. He was too preoccupied with the conversation Blaze had started with Prissy.

The dark gray tabby was asking her about her ship and where she came from. Blaze had a captivating personality and Prissy seemed to be enjoying his company.

"Coop, are you even listening to me?" Como asked, grabbing Cooper's attention.

"Why do you call him Coop? I thought his name was Cooper," Gunner wanted to know as he came up beside the two of them.

Como shrugged. "I don't know. It's just a nickname I gave him when we first met aboard the *Revenge*."

"The *Revenge*? Are you saying the two of you were on the ship before I transferred to it?" Gunner blurted out in surprise.

"That's right," Como said.

"Why did the pirates replace you, Cooper?" Gunner asked. "Don't get me wrong, I'm grateful to still be a mouser and not be stuck on some island. I was just curious why they would choose me to be the *Revenge*'s mouser when they already had you."

A sickening feeling engulfed Cooper as he debated what to say. To his horror, Como jumped in with quite an elaborate story.

"Captain Bonnet insisted on me and Cooper joining him and Captain Blackbeard on the *Queen Anne's Revenge*. Since the *Queen* is such a big ship, Cooper and Tuffy are both needed as ship's cats. Tuffy has been with Captain Blackbeard for years."

Although everything Como said was true, Cooper didn't like the idea of Gunner thinking Captain Blackbeard needed him on the ship when Tuffy had been handling the mouser duties by herself for many moons. Cooper also didn't want to tell him he was a bad omen so he remained silent.

For the rest of the journey, Cooper listened to the idle chitchat around him as he put one sand-covered paw in front of the other. A crescent moon shone above them providing very little light to guide their way.

Before long, the group came to the place where the glowing lights were located. Cooper guessed this must be the alehouse Tuffy had told him and Como about. As they drew near, his ears picked up the sound of several musical instruments playing and boisterous singing.

Cooper took a sniff around as he followed the others. The air smelled of burning wood and the stench of tobacco that he had smelled on both Captain Blackbeard and Captain Bonnet when they sometimes smoked their clay pipes late in the evenings.

By now, they were close enough for Cooper to see the remains of what appeared to be a partially torn down stone wall. Beyond it was a small building. From the glowing light emitting from the lanterns, he could see a rather large gathering under a sailcloth shelter. Some of the pirates were dancing around a campfire while others sat on old barrels and long logs eating a variety of food and drinking heavily from brown bottles.

Another group of men sat at weather-worn tables closer to the main building which was little more than a leaning shack. Based on their fancy attire, Cooper guessed these men were captains.

"Who goes there?" asked a voice in the darkness.

Tuffy and Sir Whiskers froze. Fear engulfed Cooper as he immediately started sniffing the air to see if he could detect where the voice came from. Unfortunately, it was impossible to decipher anything with so many scents in the air from the pirates.

There was some movement on top of the stone wall and seconds later a beast emerged from the dark shadows. Cooper's heart beat faster against his ribs. Was it a crocodilly? It didn't exactly look like one. The creature didn't have a long snout full of sharp teeth like the crocodilly did. Instead, it was about the length of two cats and had a short snout with a long, spiny tail.

The beast lunged off the stone wall and landed with a thud in front of Tuffy, who jumped back. It let out a hiss and flicked its spiny tail violently.

"I am the keeper of the gate. No man or beast gets by without my knowledge. I will ask you once more, who are you?"

"Hello, Gonzalo. It's me, Tuffy," the black she-cat replied. "It has been a long time since I was here. I'm Captain Blackbeard's mouser, remember? These are my friends. Blackbeard's crew brought us ashore earlier today."

"You should have spoken up faster, Tuffy. It's good to see you. Blackbeard is a legend on our island. Of course, you can pass through my gate. Welcome to Nassau," the creature said.

"You do realize there is no gate, right?" Blaze asked.

"Yes, I know, but there was a gate here for a very long time. I have guarded this spot for years and I don't plan to stop anytime soon."

"What are you?" the little spider monkey added. "You don't look like a crocodilly."

"I certainly am not a crocodile!" Gonzalo snapped. He held his rough-skinned head a little higher. "I am an iguana, but that doesn't mean I can't bite."

"We should get going, Gonzalo. Thank you for letting us pass through your gate," Tuffy said as she walked between the two stone walls where the gate must have originally been.

Prissy quickly joined the older she-cat while the macaws flew on ahead. Sir Whiskers went through next, followed by Blaze and Gunner. At last, it was Cooper and Como's turn. The two friends scampered to the other side. As they passed Gonzalo, the iguana hissed at Como causing the little monkey to grab Cooper's orange tail in fright.

"I will be keeping an eye on you, monkey," Gonzalo said.

The group left the iguana at his post as they made their way to the shack. It didn't take long to locate Captain Blackbeard, who sat at a shaky table with four other men, one of them being Captain Stede Bonnet. All four captains had obviously been drinking based on the number of bottles on the table.

Tuffy led the way up to the shelter, but stopped short of it. Her normally calm demeanor suddenly changed to uneasiness. Seconds later, a shadow emerged from the darkness surrounding the shack. This shadow turned out to be another cat.

"Well, if it isn't Teach's cat. I wondered if you would show up. Teach must have decided to let you off your grand ship for a change. You never made it onshore the last time you were here," the cat said.

Another cat joined the first. Since they were now in the light of the lanterns, Cooper could see them better. The cat who spoke was a huge, dark gray tabby with a scar over his right eye. His comrade wore a black fur coat and was missing an ear. Cooper wondered what the cat meant by calling Tuffy Teach's cat.

"I assume you are still sailing with Charles Vane," Tuffy replied.

"Yes, Captain and I get along great," the first cat continued. He leaned to one side to get a better look at Prissy, who was standing behind Tuffy. "Don't be rude, Tuffy. Aren't you going to introduce us to your friends?"

Tuffy's fur bristled, but her voice remained steady as she listed off each of their names. She then introduced the group to the two cats. Their names were Flint and Rip.

"Where are all of you off to?" Flint asked.

"You aren't welcome here," Rip quickly added.

The black cat bowed his head down in shame as Flint gave him a nasty look. His actions made Cooper wonder if Flint held some sort of command over Rip.

"Don't pay attention to him. Rip sometimes speaks before he thinks," Flint said.

"The last I heard any ship's cat was welcome on this island. Now, if you will excuse us, we need to see our captain," Tuffy replied.

Flint stepped aside as he flicked Rip with his tail, signaling for him to do the same. "Yes, of course. You go right ahead, Tuffy. I look forward to seeing you around some more, Prissy."

The group followed behind Tuffy as she approached the alehouse. Cooper didn't dare look back to see if the rogue cats were watching them, but he figured they probably were. When they were almost in the light of the lanterns, Cooper spotted Marisol and Marco flying down to meet them. Apparently seeing the two birds, Tuffy stopped and waited for them to land before speaking to the group.

"We should be far enough away from Flint so he can't hear us. I suggest that we split up so we can find the young pirate, JJ, quicker. The macaws can search the crowd from the air. Prissy, why don't you come with me. I don't want you to be alone while Flint is lurking in the shadows. He obviously wanted to know more about you in particular," she suggested.

"Do you think Flint is dangerous?" Cooper asked her.

Tuffy hesitated. "Yes, I know he is. Captain Vane's crew is a mean bunch and so are his cats. I have had numerous run-ins with

Flint. He has always been arrogant and likes to boss cats around. Unfortunately, many ship's cats willingly go along with whatever he wants."

"Why did he call you Teach's cat?" Como wanted to know.

"Flint probably heard the name Teach from his captain, Charles Vane. Most of the pirates think Captain's real name is Edward Teach. They don't know that it is a fake name he uses as a disguise. His real name is Edward Beard. The crew nicknamed him Blackbeard," Tuffy explained.

"Are you certain Flint is a threat?" Blaze asked.

Tuffy took a deep breath. "Flint is ruthless. He's the reason I only have one eye."

Without another word, the one-eyed, black cat walked away. Prissy took off behind her. The tomcats and Como stared at each other for a moment while the macaws took to the air. Then Blaze, Gunner, and Sir Whiskers went off in different directions, leaving Como and Cooper by themselves.

"I don't know about you, Como, but I don't want to split up," Cooper said.

"Me either. I'm scared of those mean cats and that iggy thing, too. I say we stick together. We make a good team," Como agreed.

"Okay, let's start right here."

The two friends walked closer to the alehouse where the four captains were talking. They got close enough to hear what they were saying, but stayed out of sight. As they crouched down behind a tropical plant, Cooper peeped out at the pirate captains.

Blackbeard leaned back in his chair and took another long swallow of whiskey. He seemed to be in the middle of telling a story about his adventures out at sea and the treasures his crew had seized. Evidently, it was a funny story because the other captains were laughing.

"But that's enough about my crew. What about ye, Paulsgrave? What have ye been up to?" Blackbeard wanted to know.

"Lately, my crew has mostly been trying to find a little peace from those annoying officers of the Royal Navy. We did have some luck a few weeks ago when we ran into a couple of French ships. They were carrying loads of new wine. My crew certainly enjoyed themselves!" the man named Paulsgrave replied.

Paulsgrave had blonde hair and a thin mustache. He wore a navy-blue coat while the pirate sitting across from him wore a long gray coat with frills around the cuffs. The second pirate had shoulder-length brown hair and a scar on the left side of his neck which he tried to cover with a red scarf.

"Williams, ye are a sly fox," the second pirate captain said, evidently referring to Paulsgrave's last name. "The Royal Navy will never catch up with ye ship."

"Ye have a point, Charles. The Navy is no match for Paulsgrave. He learned all his tricks from the best," Stede Bonnet added. "Sam Bellamy was one of the smartest pirates I've ever known. Besides ye, of course, Edward."

The gentleman pirate looked over at Blackbeard as if he wasn't sure what the tall pirate captain would say about his comment.

"Sam was one of a kind. Ye were lucky to have him as a mentor, Paulsgrave. We will all miss him," Blackbeard muttered.

"I recall the last time we were all here. Black Sam sat right over there sharing one of his long-winded stories. His stories were always the best," the other pirate who was apparently Charles Vane said.

Paulsgrave sighed. "Aye, it's hard to believe he's gone. We were such good friends. I wish my crew had been there when that storm overtook his ship. Perhaps we could have done something to help."

"Most likely, the storm would've taken ye ship to a watery grave as well," Blackbeard replied.

"I remember the day he received the nickname 'Black.' It was quite a day. Cannon fire bombarded us on all sides, but Sam was relentless. He personally kept loading the black powder into the cannon, and by the end of the day he had black powder all over him. We won the battle and the crew got a good laugh at Sam. They started calling him 'Black Sam' the same day. Ye know, I never did hear how ye got Sam's nickname," Paulsgrave said.

Blackbeard shrugged. "There isn't much to tell. We heard about Sam's shipwreck and learned that those who survived ended up hanging. My fleet began capturing ships and burning those belonging to Baltimore to avenge the death of the *Whydah*'s crew. Some of my crew started calling me 'Black' as a sort of memorial to Sam. They used to say we were alike in the way we operated our ships."

"Sam would've liked having ye named after him. He thought a lot of ye, Edward," Paulsgrave replied.

"I considered him a good friend, too. He left big boots to fill," Blackbeard continued.

"I'm not sure any of us can fill his boots. Sam will go down in history," Charles Vane added.

"Sam may not make it in a history book, but I bet his ship will. The *Whydah* was a grand ship. It may even be the largest pirate ship to ever sail these waters. Ye ship is huge too, Edward. It wouldn't surprise me if the *Queen Anne's Revenge* makes history herself," Paulsgrave mentioned.

"Aye, she's already well-known among sailors," Stede agreed. "Most of the ships we've captured are already familiar with the *Queen Anne's Revenge*. In fact, the sailors on the last ship my crew overtook were calling it Blackbeard's *Queen*."

"She's the only lady ye seem to be able to keep, Edward!" Paulsgrave joked.

Charles shook his head as he chuckled. "Edward never did have much luck with the ladies."

"I had a special lady in my life once," Blackbeard said.

The table grew silent for a few moments as the other men looked at each other.

"Are ye going to tell us her name?" Charles asked.

Blackbeard picked up the bottle in front of him and took a swallow. "It's been many years and many miles of water since then. Anyway, I'm not the only pirate known to sailors. Both of ye names have come up recently in conversations with our captives. Sounded like ye have been busy."

"Aye. My crew has been quite successful lately. Of course, times are changing and the Royal Navy is becoming a big problem. I don't know how much longer we can hold on," Paulsgrave replied.

"We will prevail if we stick together. One day we will all be legendary. Can ye imagine it? The four of us pirate friends in a history book with Sam?" Charles added.

The pirates laughed at the idea, though Cooper wondered why. It sounded like the four of them had captured many ships. Considering how the Royal Navy was after them, they had to be important.

Stede suggested a toast to “Black” Sam Bellamy’s memory. All the pirate captains lifted their bottles of whiskey together and after a few words from each of them, they collectively tilted back their heads and took a long swallow. The captains began talking about a pirate named Richard Worley when another pirate walked up. Based on his colorful patchwork coat, Cooper guessed it was Calico Jack.

Como nudged Cooper’s side. Cooper looked at his friend, realizing Como wanted to move on. The two friends left Calico and the captains as they weaved through the crowded alehouse. Everywhere Cooper looked there were groups of pirates drinking and laughing.

“Look over there, Coop,” Como said, pointing to a small group of young pirates seated around a campfire. “Maybe JJ Brooks is with those pirates.”

“Let’s go check it out,” Cooper replied.

As they approached the group, Cooper counted eleven pirates. All of them were young men and some were even boys. Cooper recalled hearing stories of fourteen-year-olds serving aboard merchant ships as cabin boys. Prior to Blackbeard’s capture, the *La Concorde* had two fifteen-year-olds who served the French captain.

The two cabin boys’ names were Louis Arot and Julien Joseph Moisant. Cooper had befriended them and had enjoyed their company, particularly when they played a game of marbles. He also felt bad for the boys since the French captain expected them to do the worst of the work and treated them harshly. Sometimes Captain Dosset even beat them.

When Blackbeard captured the ship, both boys voluntarily joined Blackbeard’s crew. They were so happy to finally be free that they told Blackbeard exactly where to find Captain Dosset’s hidden gold.

Since then, the boys had been working alongside the pirates on whatever ship Blackbeard placed them on. Cooper knew they had switched ships several times just like he had.

As Cooper looked at the faces of the young group of pirates, he recognized Louis and Julien. They were playing a game of marbles in the sand. JJ Brooks sat near the boys playing a tune on the ocarina flute while another young pirate played a Jew's harp.

"There is Marisol's flute," Cooper whispered to Como. "I can't believe we found JJ among all these pirates."

"How are we going to get it from him?" Como muttered back.

"I don't know yet, but we should get closer."

Being careful not to draw attention to themselves, the two friends skirted the group of young pirates. By the time Cooper and Como reached the other side, JJ and another young man had finished their sea chantey tune. JJ put the flute down beside him in the sand as he spoke to one of the young men who appeared to be about his age.

Cooper could hardly believe their luck. He glanced at his little monkey friend. No words passed between them, yet they both knew what they needed to do. Acting quickly but quietly, the two friends crouched down and inched their way closer.

Thankfully, it was easier to remain hidden since JJ's back was to them. The young pirate didn't even notice when Como wrapped his furry fingers around the clay flute and gently pulled it to him. Como had just picked the flute up when JJ moved.

Panicking, Cooper held his breath, unsure of what he should do to help. To his relief, JJ only leaned forward to pick something up. Glancing at Como, Cooper gave him a nod, signaling it was safe to start backing away.

Taking one step at a time, the two friends eventually got far enough away from the group of young pirates. When they were finally at a safe distance, Cooper quietly spoke up.

"We made it! I thought those pirates would catch us for sure."

Como let out a deep breath. "Me too. Marisol is going to be so excited. I guess we should see if we can find the others so they can stop looking for this flute."

"Good idea. Let's start by going—" Cooper began.

He stopped abruptly as his green eyes caught a movement. At first Cooper thought it was one of the pirates, but he quickly realized that the movement was within eye level which meant it had to be an animal. Narrowing his eyes, he squinted into the darkness hoping to see whatever it was again.

"What's wrong?" Como asked while he slipped the string of the ocarina flute around his furry neck.

"There was something moving, but I couldn't see what it was."

Before Como could respond, a cat came into view. Cooper's heart started to pound as he recognized the cat. It was Flint's friend Rip.

"Well, what do we have here?" Rip asked as multiple cats appeared behind him in the darkness. "Looks like Flint was right. Tuffy was holding out on us. Give me that trinket."

"No way!" Como shouted.

Rip chuckled, causing Cooper's fur to stand on end. "You are going to regret this."

The group of cats started to spread out. Cooper realized they were trying to trap them in. Thinking fast, he leaned closer to Como and told him to run. With a nod of understanding, the little monkey took off running in the opposite direction. Cooper stayed close behind.

Seeing their captives escaping, Rip and his friends chased Cooper and Como. Running through the darkness was nearly impossible and the further they got from the light, the harder it was to see. At some point, Cooper looked over his shoulder and discovered with relief that they had outrun the mean cats.

Suddenly, Como fell. Cooper stopped running to help him get up. Luckily, the little spider monkey didn't break Marisol's treasure, but when he tried to run again, he was limping.

"I can't run anymore, Coop. You will have to take the treasure," Como said as he lifted the bird-shaped flute from his neck and put it around Cooper's.

"But what about you?"

"I'll be fine if I can get up in the trees. Now, hurry up. Those bad kitties will be here soon. Try to get back to those crates while I see if I can get them off your trail. I will meet up with you," Como replied.

A cat came out of some bushes giving Cooper no choice but to start running again. He took off at full speed with the flute bouncing against his chest fur. Fear gripped Cooper as he zigzagged through bushes trying to confuse whoever might be behind him.

For what seemed like forever, Cooper kept running. Eventually he slowed down and looked around. Although no one was chasing him anymore, Cooper realized he had gone too far. A sickening feeling swept over him as he came to the frightening conclusion that he was alone and lost.

CHAPTER SEVEN

Nassau's Fort

Warm sunshine greeted Cooper as he woke from his sleep. He sat up and looked down at the bird-shaped flute still hanging against his chest. Realizing how exposed he was, Cooper jumped up from the hard stone surface he had been sleeping on and darted to the safety of a nearby pile of gray stones. Thoughts of crocodillies, iguanas, and other scary creatures filled his mind and increased his fear.

Cooper tried to remember how he arrived at his current location, but no matter how hard he tried, he just couldn't figure out which way he had come from. For days he had attempted to find his way back to the town only to become lost. The maze of tropical trees and undergrowth made the task of returning to town worse.

Things did get a little hopeful late last night when Cooper stumbled upon a strange stone structure. Exhausted from his trek in the bushes, Cooper must have drifted off to sleep despite his efforts to stay alert. Now that it was daylight, he noticed the structure was some type of abandoned building. Based on the fallen piles of stones, he figured it had been a very long time since any humans had lived here.

Knowing he had to find a way back to the ship, Cooper reluctantly left the safety of the stone pile. Taking a few deep breaths, he attempted to keep himself calm as he explored the ruins. At one point he even jumped up on the ledge of a half-broken wall to see if he could see better from a higher vantage point. Nothing in the horizon seemed familiar.

Deciding he needed to get higher than the wall, Cooper summoned his courage, shook his haunches, and pounced to the next ledge. After three more pounces, he was walking on top of the highest part of the stone structure. The stones arched in the middle to form a doorway. Up here, it looked like a giant stone fort.

Holding his tail high to help him balance, Cooper inched his way around the narrow stonework of the fort's wall. The fort stood at the end of a peninsula surrounded by sandy beaches and the ocean on three sides. To the south, the land was green with trees and undergrowth, but in the distance, Cooper could see a town. He guessed it was Nassau.

Relieved to know where the town was, he wondered how much time it would take to reach it. The town looked far away. Could he make it by dark or would he have to spend the night alone again?

Sighing, Cooper tried not to get upset about his circumstances. He looked up at the brilliant blue sky dotted with small, puffy white clouds and reminded himself he wasn't alone. The Mighty Creator was with him and would help him get back to his friends. He just had to keep believing.

Feeling hopeful, Cooper slowly descended the stone wall. By the time he made it to the final wall, he cautiously looked around and sniffed the air to make sure there were no dangerous animals nearby.

With the flute hanging around his neck, Cooper jumped down to the stone-covered ground and set off on his journey for Nassau. He barely made it through the maze of the stone structure when a flash of pink caught his eye.

Cooper paused to look around, but didn't see anything. Shaking his head, Cooper told himself he was imagining things. He started walking again when his green eyes spotted another pink flash.

"Hello there!" exclaimed a voice.

Fearful, Cooper spun around to see who had spoken. To his amazement, he found himself staring at some sort of pink bird. This bird was a lot taller than any Cooper had ever seen. It had long, stick-like legs and bright, pinkish-red feathers. The bird also had a long curvy neck that could reach all the way to its black, webbed feet.

"I'm so glad I found you, cat. Everyone is out looking for you," the pink bird said.

"Who are you?" Cooper asked.

"Sorry, I should've introduced myself. I'm Annarose. Gonzalo the iguana told us you were missing and gave us a description. It's a good thing your fur is orange so we could easily find you."

The bird's comment surprised Cooper. For once his orange fur came in handy. Maybe being an orange cat wasn't bad after all.

"How do you know the iguana?" Cooper added.

"Everyone knows Gonzalo, he's the keeper of the gate."

Cooper felt a bit overwhelmed. "I can't believe Gonzalo told you about me. How did he even know I needed help?"

"It's the strangest story I've ever heard. Gonzalo said he was doing his nightly rounds when he ran into a frantic little spider monkey. The monkey was looking for a group of cats and two tropical birds. After Gonzalo helped the monkey find his friends, the whole group started looking for you. When morning arrived, Gonzalo came down to the beach where my flock lives. He told us what happened and asked for our help. My flock agreed to help with the search and I decided to come look up here."

"I'm glad you did. It's a relief to run into someone who knows their way around the island. By the way, what kind of bird are you?"

The bird laughed. "I'm a flamingo. You are lucky to have so many good friends. Come on, I'll show you the way to the beach. It will be much easier to walk on the damp sand."

Cooper followed the strange, pink bird away from the stone fort. The pink-feathered flamingo strutted along beside Cooper, asking him questions about his disappearance. Starting with the search for Marisol's lost treasure, Cooper recounted what happened to him and Como. He then talked about the rogue pirate cats and their determination to get the clay flute.

Annarose had apparently heard about the pirate cats. She made a few comments about their leader, Flint, and how his cat crew were ruining the island by scaring the existing animals and even killing a few who stood up to them. Stunned by this news, Cooper started to ask her more about Flint when Annarose announced they had arrived at the sand dunes.

The pink flamingo briefly took to the air. She landed at the top of the nearest sand dune and encouraged Cooper to join her. This proved to be a difficult task. With every attempt to walk up the sandy hill, Cooper slid back down again. Annarose kept offering suggestions, but none seemed to help. Finally, Cooper had an idea.

Backing away from the giant hill of sand, Cooper gave himself a running start. As his paws met the sand, he clawed his way up the dune spinning sand behind him. It took a lot of effort, but he eventually made it to the top.

Exhausted, Cooper caught his breath as he peered over the sea grass growing at the top of the dune. The beach below was pink with hundreds of flamingos. Oddly, many were standing on one leg.

"I'm going down to my flock to tell them I found you, Cooper," Annarose said.

"Why are so many of them standing on one leg?" Cooper asked.

"It's just something we do. I'm not sure why. Anyway, go ahead and start walking down to the beach. I'll catch up to you."

Cooper slid down the sand dune as the flamingo stretched out her pink-feathered wings and descended gracefully to her flock. Once Cooper was at the bottom of the hill, he started walking away from the flamingos, wondering how they could stand on one leg without falling over. He hadn't walked very far when Annarose flew overhead and landed next to him.

Together, they made their way across the damp sand at the edge of the water, dodging the incoming waves rushing ashore. As they walked, Annarose shared stories about her flock.

They were almost at the opposite end of the island when Cooper noticed something at the top of the sand dunes. At first, he didn't know what it was, but as he continued to listen to Annarose, he realized the object was following them.

"Annarose," Cooper softly interrupted his new friend. "I think we're being followed."

"What? By whom?" the flamingo asked, looking around.

As if her question had summoned them, a group of cats suddenly appeared at the top of the sand dunes. Cooper's stomach felt queasy as he recognized the leader of the group. It was Flint's mean sidekick, Rip.

Realizing there was no need to hide anymore, Rip yelled at his fellow comrades, instructing them to grab Cooper and the treasure still dangling from his neck. Cooper instinctively started running. Annarose took to the air, flying over Cooper and giving him updates on how close the rogue cats were.

Gasping for air, Cooper tried to keep from falling on the slippery sand. Despite his efforts, the rogue cats seemed to be gaining on him. Eventually, Cooper could see the alehouses up ahead.

"Keep it up, Cooper! You've almost made it," Annarose said.

In no time, Cooper arrived at one of the alehouses. He slowed his pace, thinking the rogue cats would leave him alone, but he was wrong. Wondering what he should do now, Cooper was pleasantly surprised when Gonzalo appeared from behind his stone wall.

"You found him!" the iguana exclaimed, apparently speaking to Annarose. "I knew it was a good idea to get your flock involved."

"We can't talk now, we're being chased," Annarose replied.

"Chased?" Gonzalo repeated as he raised his head a bit higher to see better. "Why, that's Rip! How dare he come into my territory threatening other animals. Get behind my wall. I'll deal with these hateful cats."

Cooper scrambled behind the wall as Annarose landed beside him. Meanwhile, Gonzalo faced Rip and his crew of cats. Although Cooper couldn't hear everything that Gonzalo said to the rogue cats, it was clear they didn't want to cross him. Surprisingly, Rip backed away with only verbal threats directed at Cooper.

Once the rogue cats had trotted off, Gonzalo turned to Cooper and Annarose. "They'll be back. Rip is probably on his way to find Flint as we speak. Flint won't give up so easily. You need to get moving, cat. The pirates have been packing up their things all day. I told Tuffy I would send you their way if my friends found you."

"Are you saying the pirates are leaving?" Cooper asked in panic.

"It appears they are, but perhaps they are only preparing to leave. You should hurry, you might make it to the pier before the last boat rows out to the ships," the iguana said.

"I'll go with you to the pier just in case those mean cats return or in case your friends have left you behind," Annarose added.

"Thanks," Cooper replied. "I won't forget you, Gonzalo. You have been a great friend."

The iguana grinned. "You are welcome to pass through my gate anytime you return to our island. May the winds be at your back."

With a dip of his head, Cooper trotted away from Gonzalo and his wall. Annarose flew overhead, keeping an eye out for Rip and his crew of mean cats. As Cooper drew closer to the beach, his nervousness grew. Unfortunately, things didn't look so good as his green eyes spotted the pier down by the seashore. A solitary periauger bumped against the end of the dock.

Cooper's heart sank as his orange paws crossed the sandy beach. The massive piles of cargo brought to shore from the five pirate ships were no longer there. He looked out in the harbor to see if he could spot *Queen Anne's Revenge* and her fleet, but with so many other ships anchored in the cove, it was difficult to see if they had left the island.

Coming to a stop near the water's edge, Cooper tried not to panic. Feelings of despair washed over him as he debated what to do. He was so upset, he jumped when Annarose spoke to him.

"I didn't mean to startle you, Cooper. I thought you should know we have company headed our way," the flamingo said as she tilted her long neck to one side, pointing in the direction of the newcomer.

Immediately concerned, Cooper relaxed when he recognized the cat walking up to them. The cat had long, thick black fur and yellow eyes. It was Sir Whiskers.

"Shiver me whiskers! I can't believe it's you, Cooper," the graying cat exclaimed. "We looked all over this island for you. Even Captain Bonnet was frantically searching every shack and crate. Everyone was terribly upset when Captain Blackbeard announced they were going to have to leave you behind. That poor little monkey cried like a newborn kitten. Those pirates really struggled to force him into his cage. He bit several of them."

"Why haven't the pirates taken you back to your ship? I assume they haven't set sail yet," Cooper asked.

"No, Captain Blackbeard had some things to attend to first. He held a meeting right here on the beach yesterday afternoon. Every man in the fleet had a choice to stay with Blackbeard or collect their share of the communal plunder," Sir Whiskers replied.

"What is communal plunder?" Annarose interrupted.

"The pirates keep stolen treasure in a general pile called the communal plunder. From what I understand, the quartermaster oversees the inventory so the captain will know how much plunder to give the crew when they split company. Most of this is new to me.

Since I'm the ship's cat for the *Land of Promise*, I didn't know much about pirates until recently," Sir Whiskers told her.

"So back to my question. Shouldn't you be on it?" Cooper hinted.

Sir Whiskers chuckled. "No, my friend, the *Land of Promise* will not be joining Blackbeard's fleet. Hundreds of pirates decided to stay behind. Some said they wanted to retire from piracy to live a life of ease while others plan to join smaller pirate crews or start their own. The few remaining crew members of the *Land of Promise* have decided to stay on the island, so naturally I will stay here with them."

"How many pirates are staying?" Annarose asked.

"I don't know exactly. Surprisingly, there were pirates from other crews who asked Blackbeard if they could join up with him. I don't think Captain Blackbeard really wanted to grow the fleet after shrinking it down to four ships, but one of the men seemed to be a former friend of his. There were about seven hundred pirates originally and now only around four hundred. I know this because those who were joining had to sign papers."

"Sign papers?" Cooper blurted out in surprise.

"They had to swear allegiance to Blackbeard's fleet. Pirates are interesting creatures. I had no idea they had so many rules. I'm ashamed to say Captain Blackbeard seems more structured and fairer than my own captain. He never gave our crew choices like Blackbeard has done, and he certainly would never allow them to vote on things," Sir Whiskers said.

"I have never heard anyone say that pirates are fair. Most of the ones I've seen here on the island are crooks. This Blackbeard fellow must be different somehow," Annarose replied.

"Speaking of Blackbeard, here he comes now," Sir Whiskers added as he nodded toward the dock.

Cooper spun around just in time to see the tall, bearded captain step up on the wooden boards of the dock with two other men. One of them was the third-ranking crew member, Thomas Miller. Cooper didn't recognize the other man and wondered if he was one of the new pirates Sir Whiskers talked about.

As the three pirates walked to the end of the dock, Cooper realized the Mighty Creator was giving him an opportunity. This may be his only chance of getting back on *Queen Anne's Revenge*. For a split second he debated whether he even wanted to return to life as a ship's cat. The thought quickly passed as he felt Marisol's treasure hanging against his chest. He had to somehow get back on the ship.

"I better get going before Blackbeard leaves the island. This is my chance," Cooper said to his new friends.

"Are you serious?" Sir Whiskers gasped. "Those pirates are climbing aboard the periauger now. There is no way you will make it."

Cooper looked back at the dock. Thomas and the other pirate were already in the periauger. Blackbeard handed them something he had been carrying. He then grabbed hold of the piling as he swung his leg into the boat.

"I must try. My friends are counting on me," Cooper replied.

"Good luck, Cooper! If you ever return to Nassau come see me. You can always find my flock at the end of the island," Annarose said as she ruffled her pretty, pink feathers.

"Safe travels, my friend," Sir Whiskers added with a flick of his tail and a dip of his head.

"Goodbye to both of you, and thanks for everything!" Cooper

exclaimed as he took off in the direction of the dock.

Running in the sand was difficult, but Cooper didn't let it stop him. By the time his paws touched the wooden boards of the dock, the pirates were pushing away from the pier. A sickening feeling overwhelmed Cooper as the pirates picked up their oars and started to row the boat into the sea. He sunk his claws into the wood to gain traction as he darted down the pier.

Breathless, Cooper came to an abrupt stop at the end of the dock with nowhere else to go. Pacing back and forth, he watched in horror as Blackbeard and his comrades dipped their oars in and out of the greenish-blue water about a boat length away from him.

Suddenly an idea came to Cooper. Knowing fear would creep up on him if he dwelled on this idea, Cooper didn't wait. He ran back down the pier a short distance, then turned around and took off running as fast as his paws would carry him. When he reached the end, he lunged off the pier praying he would land in the boat.

Cooper's claws scraped the outer wooden surface of the periauger, but unfortunately, he found himself landing with a splash in the sea. Scrambling to stay above the water, Cooper meowed loudly in hopes to get his captain's attention. His efforts paid off as Captain Blackbeard turned around.

"Well, what do ye know? It's Cooper!" Blackbeard exclaimed as he leaned over the edge of the periauger and grabbed Cooper by the scruff of his neck. "Ye sure got into a mess, didn't ye?"

Blackbeard plucked Cooper out of the sea and held him over the side of the boat while Cooper's fur dripped with water. Although he despised being wet and didn't enjoy the rough grip of Blackbeard's fingers at the back of his neck, Cooper was grateful the pirate captain saved him.

“How did that runt get in the water?” Thomas Miller asked.

“I think he jumped off the pier,” the new pirate replied.

Blackbeard chuckled as he put Cooper in the bottom of the boat between his big, black boots. “This cat is tougher than I thought. He’s been sort of a scaredy-cat compared to Tuffy, but I suppose I underestimated him.”

“Don’t tell me he’s a ship’s cat,” the new pirate said. “Since when do ye allow an orange cat on ye ship? Ye know they are a bad omen.”

“He was the ship’s cat before we took *Queen Anne’s Revenge*. Stede insisted we keep him. Looks like he’s a brave pirate cat after all.”

“What’s around his neck?” Thomas asked.

Not wanting to give up the bird-shaped trinket, Cooper let out a hiss. The reaction made Blackbeard pull his hand back.

“Guess he doesn’t want us to find out. Let’s get going.”

Thomas and the other pirate picked up the oars once more as Captain Blackbeard settled at the back of the periauger. Shivering in his soggy orange fur, Cooper sat tall and proud between his captain’s boots. He had succeeded and was on his way to Blackbeard’s *Queen*.

 CHAPTER EIGHT 

Stormy Seas

Adjusting to life back at sea had been somewhat difficult. Although Cooper had grown to like life on a ship, he still struggled with his duties as the ship's mouser, particularly when it came to fighting those dreadful rats. Cooper had hoped his bad luck had changed since he managed to return to *Queen Anne's Revenge* with the bird-shaped flute, but unfortunately, the young pirate, JJ Brooks, had taken it from Cooper as soon as he arrived on board. Thankfully, Marisol was just happy that Cooper had made it back to the ship, and was confident they would be able to get her treasure back at some point.

The rest of the crew were having a difficult time as well. In less than a week after Captain Blackbeard had ordered the fleet to pull up their anchors and set sail, many of the men suddenly fell ill. This unusual situation caused a lot of chaos among the crews of the four ships since the pirates who were healthy had double the number of duties to fulfill. The French surgeon Blackbeard pressed into service from a previously captured ship tried to help the sick men, but so far, he was unable to cure them from the sickness.

With many of the pirates lying sick in their hammocks below

deck, Tuffy had taken on even more responsibility above deck. She insisted that she and Cooper had a duty to help Captain Blackbeard do something he couldn't accomplish by himself. The captain needed them to be lookouts.

Tuffy had explained to Cooper how important it was for them to keep an eye on the French surgeon in case he turned on them. It was equally important to spend more time eavesdropping on the members of the crew who could still work, to make sure a mutiny wasn't about to break out.

Cooper, who wasn't familiar with mutinies, was glad when his spider monkey friend asked what a mutiny was. To their horror, they learned a mutiny was when a riot broke out resulting in a takeover of the ship. After hearing this, Como offered to help eavesdrop on the crew, too.

Today had started out as usual with Cooper assisting Tuffy in their shared duties of searching out rats and mice in the bottom of the ship. By noon, the two cats had captured and killed more than a dozen mice and had only encountered one rat, which suited Cooper just fine. Cooper was feeling very pleased with how well the day was going when Tuffy walked up to him with a strange look on her face.

"What's wrong?" Cooper asked the older she-cat as he dropped a dead mouse at the foot of the stairs leading to the deck above them.

"You don't feel it?"

"Feel what?"

"Stay still a moment and concentrate, Cooper."

Cooper tried, but he wasn't sure what he was supposed to be concentrating on. He was about to tell Tuffy this when a prickle went down his spine causing him to shiver.

"You felt it then, didn't you?" Tuffy hinted. "Something is going to happen. I can feel it in my bones. We better get up on deck and see what's going on."

"What do you think will happen?" Cooper asked in alarm.

"I don't know for sure. Feels like a storm is brewing."

Tuffy picked up a mouthful of mice and carried them upstairs. Cooper did the same as fearful thoughts crept into his mind. At the top of the stairs, Cooper spotted the French doctor leaning over a sick sailor who was moaning in misery. The doctor wore an odd outfit compared to the pirates and spoke with a thick accent. He had a thin brown mustache and a little bit of hair on his chin.

Cooper remembered seeing a man back home in France with similar facial hair. His mother had said it was silly for a human man to trim his beard to look like a goat. Thinking about this made Cooper smile. He missed his dear mother and all the wise things she had taught him. What would she think of him being a pirate cat?

Lost in his thoughts, Cooper accidentally bumped into Tuffy's backside as she stooped to drop her fresh kill. Embarrassed, Cooper immediately dropped his own mouthful of mice on the pile.

"I'm so sorry, Tuffy," he apologized.

"You need to stay alert and stop daydreaming."

Cooper folded his ears back in shame as Tuffy trotted to the other end of the sleeping quarters. Her words stung his heart, but Cooper felt like she didn't mean to be harsh. The one-eyed she-cat seemed distracted herself. It was almost like she wasn't even the same cat. Her odd behavior worried Cooper. Apparently, Tuffy's instincts were telling her more than she was saying.

Passing multiple hammocks of sick pirates, the two cats made their way to the galley. Blackbeard's faithful friend Cookie stood at the table preparing the next meal. To Cooper's surprise, he was busily plucking feathers off a headless chicken.

"Goodness! I hope that wasn't Henrietta or Rooney," Cooper gasped as he stared wide-eyed at the pool of blood and feathers on the floor.

"Don't worry about them. Cookie knows better than to kill our best hen and rooster. Come on, let's go find Captain."

As if her words had summoned him, Captain Blackbeard came down into the galley. Cookie greeted him with a joke about a headless ghost chicken, but Blackbeard didn't seem to be in a joking mood.

"What's ailing ye?" Cookie asked.

"John Martin just informed me that the other ship we were planning to capture surrendered to Israel Hands and the crew of the *Adventure*. Their captain is Leigh Ashworth," Blackbeard said.

"Ashworth? Isn't he a pirate?"

"Aye, he sailed with the Old Flying Gang, remember? Vane told me Ashworth retired, but perhaps he has started back. I sent word for him to come aboard so I can talk to him."

"I forgot about him sailing with us when we were part of Benjamin Hornigold's gang. It's hard to recall all the pirates who sailed with Captain Hornigold. There were so many ships, and crews were always changing. Anyway, the men won't be happy. This makes the second ship we've tried to plunder that turned out to be a former pirate."

Blackbeard sighed. "I know. William told me several men had complained to him about me paying Josiah Burgess the other day for the supplies he had on his ship. They don't understand how the pirate rules work. Burgess was with the Old Flying Gang at one point, too. Just because he's changing his piracy status doesn't mean we have the right to plunder their ship. Pirates are supposed to live by a code."

"Ye can't tell these young lads anything. They think they know more than we do. We've been at this for two years. Times are changing, Edward. We've been places they have yet to see and have done things they don't have the guts to do. These lads lack common sense and respect. Just think what would've happened if we hadn't lived by rules. We'd be dead by now," Cookie said.

"Dying by the sword sounds pretty good compared to dying from that disease the men are getting. Those men are miserable," Blackbeard continued as he pointed toward the sleeping quarters.

Cookie shook his head. "I hate it for the poor fellows."

"I'm concerned for the rest of us, too. Honestly, I haven't been feeling well myself. Although I haven't been sleeping well lately with all these problems on my mind."

"Aye. 'Tis hard to sleep with the weight of the world on ye shoulders. Does the doctor think the sickness will spread?"

"It could," answered a voice.

Everyone, including Tuffy and Cooper, turned to see who had spoken. To Cooper's surprise, the voice belonged to the French doctor, who was now standing in the doorway wiping his hands on the cream-colored apron tied around his waist.

"May I have a word with you, Monsieur?" he asked Blackbeard.

"Whatever ye need to say can be said in front of Cookie," the bearded captain replied.

The Frenchman nervously glanced at Cookie. "As you wish. I

cannot do much to help your crew. They need special medicine which I do not have on this ship."

"If ye had this special medicine, would they survive?" Blackbeard wanted to know.

"Perhaps. Their chances would be much better, but I cannot make promises. There are a few who may be too far gone to save."

"Where can we get such medicine?"

"A major port would have them."

"Such as Charles Town?"

The Frenchman hesitated. "*Oui*, I would think so."

"Very well, then. As soon as I meet with Captain Ashworth and get things straight with him, I will tell the men to set a course for the southern Carolinas. In the meantime, get working on a list of the medicines," Blackbeard said.

"These medicines are quite expensive," the French doctor replied.

Blackbeard chuckled. "There's no need to worry about that. Just make me a list."

The French doctor dipped his head in understanding as he retreated to the sleeping quarters. Once he was gone, Cookie turned to his captain.

"How are ye going to get medicine from Charles Town without alerting the government, Edward? Ye can't sail up the channel. There will be pilots on the islands who will send word to their governor. Charles Town is a major port and it will be heavily guarded."

"I don't plan to sail up to the docks, but I do think our chances of getting what we want will be good. Once I talk to Leigh Ashworth, I'll have a better idea of what we're dealing with. I'm guessing he was recently in Charles Town himself just like Josiah Burgess."

A stomping sound echoed in the stairway, followed by a loud shriek. Cooper immediately knew the shriek belonged to Como.

"Get away from me, ye foolish monkey!" a man shouted as he staggered into the galley dragging Como along.

The little spider monkey was holding onto the man's leg attempting to bite him. Surprisingly, the man was able to pry Como's arms away from his leg only to have Como jump on his head. This prompted Captain Blackbeard to step in.

"Alright, monkey, if ye can't behave ye will be thrown overboard," he grunted as he grabbed Como and roughly yanked him off the other pirate.

"Looks like that monkey whipped ye butt, John!" Cookie laughed.

The pirate named John ran his fingers through his black hair to tame it down while Blackbeard put Como back on the floor. As soon as Como was free again, he made another lunge at the pirate. Blackbeard was too fast for him though.

"I told ye to leave John alone," Blackbeard snapped as he grabbed Como. "I don't want to punish ye, monkey, but I will not put up with an unruly crew whether they are men or animals."

"Those animals can't understand ye," John said.

Blackbeard sighed. "Well, I don't know about the monkey or the macaws, but I truly believe Tuffy understands me, at least she acts like she does. I've never had any trouble with her."

Tuffy seemed to stand a little straighter when her captain mentioned her name. Meanwhile, Como screeched in protest as Blackbeard put him under his arm to control the wild little monkey.

"Como," Tuffy hissed. "Pull yourself together! You should know better than to attack a member of the crew. John Martin is Captain's friend. They knew each other before they became pirates."

"That meanie pirate stepped on my tail. What was I supposed to do? Let him get by with it?" Como replied sharply.

"Well, you shouldn't have bit him."

"Oh, I only nipped at his leg. He'll live."

Blackbeard wrestled Como until he managed to wrap his arms around the monkey's body. "I better put him in his cage for a while."

"That reminds me of why I was coming down here in the first place," John said. "Captain Leigh Ashworth has arrived. Stede Bonnet took him to ye cabin. William Howard asked me to come get ye while he tries to keep Stede from embarrassing us. Thomas Miller is talking with the men Ashworth brought along."

"Let's get up there then," Blackbeard replied. "Cookie, keep an eye on the surgeon. I don't trust that Frenchman."

"Ye can count on me, Edward. I don't trust him either."

John started up the stairs while Blackbeard followed carrying the shrieking spider monkey. Tuffy scampered behind them, calling out to Cooper to hurry up so they wouldn't miss meeting the new pirate captain. As soon as they stepped out on the main deck, Cooper folded down his ears. Thick, dark clouds hung low in the sky, threatening to dump rain at any moment as a brisk wind blew in from the north. Another shiver went down Cooper's spine as he looked up at them. Tuffy's instincts had been right. A storm was brewing.

Even the pirates seemed concerned as they worked to take down the massive cloth sails. Although the hemp-made cloth was stiff with tar, their durability was no match for the powerful winds a storm could produce.

As Cooper scurried across the deck behind Tuffy, he couldn't help but feel afraid. His fear only got worse as he spotted four strangers talking to Blackbeard's third officer in command, Thomas Miller. Cooper guessed these were the men of Captain Ashworth's crew who had rowed him over to the *Queen Anne's Revenge* on their periauger.

John Martin held open the door to the captain's cabin so Blackbeard could enter the cabin first. Tuffy didn't waste any time going with him. The one-eyed she-cat swiftly maneuvered around Blackbeard's boots as she followed the men inside. Cooper quickly joined her just as John closed the door.

Tuffy slipped under the straight-backed chair in the corner of the cabin while Blackbeard took Como into Stede Bonnet's sleeping quarters, presumably to put him into his cage. Cooper felt sorry for his little friend, but he didn't dare try to free him when the fearsome captain Blackbeard was the one who put him there. Como would just have to wait awhile.

Squatting beside Tuffy, Cooper got comfortable as he took in the scenery from this new vantage point. An agitated-looking William Howard leaned against Blackbeard's desk with his arms crossed while Stede Bonnet attempted to entertain Captain Ashworth with Marisol and Marco. Both macaws were squawking as Stede tugged on their tail feathers.

"Welcome aboard, Leigh," Blackbeard said as Stede put Marco and Marisol on the wooden chest that sat behind the desk.

William looked relieved to see Blackbeard as Captain Ashworth stood to shake hands with him. The short, brown-haired captain wore a burgundy coat and was missing a leg. In its place was a wooden peg which enabled him to stand up. Cooper noticed that one of his hands was missing, too.

"It's good to see ye, Captain Teach," Ashworth replied. "I was concerned when my men told me they spotted four ships, but we got lucky. Ye have always treated us fairly, Edward, and I want to thank ye for not shooting cannons at us."

"Why would we do a thing like that?" Stede Bonnet asked.

Blackbeard sent him a nasty look as he interrupted him. "Why don't ye get out the brandy, Stede. Let's enjoy a little dram while we talk, shall we?"

Stede hurried to get a bright green glass bottle from the shelf while William grabbed some pewter cups. As they offered their guest the brandy, Blackbeard asked Ashworth to explain what he meant.

"There's been a few of our former comrades who don't approve of my decision to retire from piracy. I'm trying to run a legitimate merchant company here, at least as far as the government thinks. I may be smuggling some things under their noses, but I still wish to stay out of their reach when it comes to hanging. I have my papers and so does the rest of my crew."

"Are these former comrades anyone I know?" Blackbeard asked.

Ashworth nodded. "Aye. We've had several run-ins. Even with Charles Vane, although Vane didn't seem to be as threatening as his crew. When Charles called me to come aboard his ship, it was his quartermaster, Calico Jack Rackham, who did most of the talking and threatening. Charles better watch his back. If his crew doesn't vote him out of his captain position in the next six months, Calico might take matters into his own hands and get rid of him in other ways."

"An unruly crew is certainly a bad situation for a captain to deal with," Blackbeard agreed. "We saw Vane at Nassau just a few days ago. He didn't mention any trouble, but what captain would admit such to his peers? Paulsgrave Williams was also there along with some members of Benjamin Hornigold's Old Flying Gang."

"I heard there was some trouble among the Flying Gang as well," Ashworth said.

"That's true," John Martin replied. "It's the reason I rejoined Blackbeard's crew. I don't agree with the way things are. Pirates used to believe the same things and now it's every man for himself."

"Unfortunately, John's right. Most of us started out as privateers working for the government to take on enemies of the Crown. I can't tell ye how many Spanish ships my crew has captured over the years and plundered for the benefit of the British. Honestly, I didn't mind it at first. It was our duty to defend Queen Anne's rule, but when she died and that impostor, King George, took over, things were never the same," Blackbeard said.

"I agree, Edward. I didn't even know that King George had given orders to stop plundering the Spaniards. The next thing I knew, the Royal Navy was hunting us. King George shouldn't be king, he's German and can't even speak English. He doesn't care how much treasure we seized and handed over to the Lords Proprietors. Just think how rich we would be if we had kept all the treasure," Ashworth added.

Blackbeard chuckled. "Aye, we would be able to live a life a luxury. No more sweaty days tarring the ship or worrying if a hurricane is coming. We wouldn't have to meet the desires of crews or spend hours trying to outsmart the Royal Navy. Life would be sweet!"

"If ye had the royal pardon like I do, ye could at least relax when the Royal Navy sails within view."

"Royal pardon, eh? Did ye get it in Charles Town?" Blackbeard wanted to know.

"We did. My entire crew received one from their governor. All ye do is swear to refrain from further piracy and sign ye name to the document. Of course, a little gold helps! A sack of it will buy ye as many pardons as ye need with no questions asked."

"Interesting. Well, since ye ship just left Charles Town with fresh supplies, would ye consider selling us the cargo?" Blackbeard hinted.

"Maybe, but then I will have to go back to Charles Town to restock. My crew was wanting to go down to the tropics."

"I understand. The thing is, we are getting low on supplies. We are still on the run though, so we can't sail up to the docks at Charles Town to restock. I know ye need supplies too, but ye have the freedom to go back to town since ye have pardons. Just tell the townsfolk that pirates captured ye ship. After all, it would be the truth."

"Alright, ye have a deal. I'll sell ye the supplies for a good price," Ashworth said as he and Blackbeard shook hands.

"Excellent! Let's have another round of brandy, Stede," Blackbeard said, as he motioned for his so-called co-captain to pour some more brandy from the bright green bottle.

By now the ship seemed to be rocking back and forth more so than usual. Cooper thought he was imagining things, but apparently Blackbeard had noticed it, too. The tall pirate captain leaned closer to his friend John and muttered something about checking the weather conditions. Blackbeard then snapped his fingers.

"Okay, Cooper, it's time for us to do our rounds," Tuffy said.

"Our rounds?"

"Yes, Captain just sent me the message by snapping his fingers together. That's my signal. He wants us to go with John. Let's go."

Confused, Cooper followed Tuffy out of hiding. The two of them headed for the door as John stepped out on deck. A powerful force of wind greeted them, causing both Cooper and Tuffy to brace themselves by unsheathing their claws. Worry engulfed Cooper at the sight of the nearly black sky. The storm seemed to be coming on strong as Blackbeard's *Queen* rocked from side to side with the rolling waves. Meanwhile, big raindrops began to fall from the dark clouds.

Dreading the aspect of getting wet, Cooper followed Tuffy across the deck. He wished he didn't have the responsibilities of a ship's cat, but he also knew his captain was counting on him. All he could do was keep praying that the Mighty Creator would bring them safely through the storm. Unfortunately, the nasty weather wasn't the only stormy seas headed their way. Blackbeard's plan to blockade Charles Town would surely rock the colony as well.

 CHAPTER NINE 

The Blockade

Seagulls swooped through the cloth sails seemingly laughing at the pirate crew working hard down below. Cooper watched the seagulls from his perch at the bow of the ship. The sunshine felt good against his orange fur, especially after so many days of nonstop rain. It was one of the only good things that had taken place in the last several days.

Thankfully the fleet of ships survived the storm without any major damages; however, the rough seas caused a lot of tension within the ranks of pirates. After Captain Leigh Ashworth had returned to his ship, *Ann*, Blackbeard called a meeting with his top-ranked pirates both on the *Queen Anne's Revenge* and on the other ships.

Their discussion was intense. Some wanted to go down to the southernmost peninsula of the colonies where treasure ships had wrecked so they could dive for the treasures underwater. Others agreed with Blackbeard's plan to blockade the port of Charles Town. The bad weather forced their meeting to be short, which was fine until Blackbeard decided to go with his plan anyway. His decision made many of the pirates angry.

Still, enough of Blackbeard's four-hundred-pirate crew stood by him to carry out his orders to sail up to Charles Town. Within days, the fleet of ships had arrived at the inlet that led to the port. About nine miles from the town itself, they spread out over the sandbar and waited for their prey.

It didn't take long for ships to start sailing into their trap. The prospect of capturing these prize ships excited every crew member which helped Blackbeard's reputation. Cooper was relieved that things had gotten better with the crew, especially since it was now his job to watch out for potential takeovers alone.

Unfortunately, the stormy winds ripped one of the main sails in half, which caused quite a commotion among the crew of *Queen Anne's Revenge* during the middle of the storm. In the chaos, several of the pirates received injuries. One pirate ended up tangled in the sails and somehow tripped on a rope, causing him to fall on top of Tuffy. The incident wounded the she-cat's back leg and forced her to stay in Blackbeard's cabin for the last three days.

Tuffy's injury led to a conflict among the pirate crew. Many felt it was a bad omen and were blaming Blackbeard. Although Cooper certainly didn't think it was Captain Blackbeard's fault, the idea of Tuffy's injury being a bad omen did bother him. After all, things had been going badly ever since.

Thankfully, Cookie seemed to think Tuffy would make a full recovery, but until she was stronger, it was up to Cooper to take on the sole duties of a ship's cat. The weight of this task was heavy on Cooper's heart. More than anything, he wanted to make Tuffy proud and be a ship's cat Captain Blackbeard could count on.

From his point of view at the bow of the ship, Cooper could see

Captain Blackbeard standing on the quarterdeck with his spyglass in hand. Cooper looked in the same direction, noticing another ship was heading their way from the port of Charles Town.

Feeling an uncomfortable prickle go down his spine, Cooper decided he better go warn Blackbeard or at least try to. Jumping down from his perch, he skirted the railing of the ship, doing his best to stay out of the way of the pirates as someone rang the bell hanging at the back of the ship.

"Look alive, men!" Blackbeard hollered from the quarterdeck. "There is another ship coming. This one is sailing out of the inlet. Prepare to capture the ship and send word to the crews of the *Revenge*, *Adventure*, and *Adventure II*."

"Aye, aye, Captain!" chanted the crew as they got to work.

Cooper had almost made it to the staircase leading up to the quarterdeck when he spotted his little monkey friend swinging from the ropes and sails up in the rigging. He paused to watch Como do a flip when a voice startled him.

"Arrrr! There ye are, ye worthless cat!" the pirate shouted as he made a grab for Cooper.

Stunned, Cooper scampered up the stairs as fast as his paws would take him. He made it to the top of the quarterdeck and skidded to a halt right in front of Blackbeard. The fearsome pirate captain reached down to pick Cooper up just as the other pirate caught up to him.

"Why are ye chasing Cooper, Owen? Ye should be helping ye fellow comrades prepare to capture the prize ships," Blackbeard asked, holding Cooper in the crook of his elbow.

"That cat is failing his duties. Ye should throw him overboard!"

"Is that so? Well, walk with me and tell me why ye are so upset," Blackbeard replied as he went downstairs carrying Cooper.

Clearly frustrated, Owen followed Blackbeard and Cooper to the captain's cabin. As they walked, Owen told his captain that he and John Giles had gone down into the hold to fetch Cookie a few barrels of food. They discovered rats actively eating some of the food supply.

"Tuffy wouldn't have allowed this to happen. Either Cooper does his job or he gets punished," Owen said as they entered the cabin.

Evidently hearing her name, Tuffy lifted her head from the little bed Cookie had made for her in the corner of the room. Across the cabin, Marco and Marisol ruffled their brightly colored tail feathers as they flew to their new perch on the back of Blackbeard's chair.

"I appreciate ye concerns, but I'll be the judge of who deserves punishment on this ship. We need a ship's cat and right now Cooper is all we've got," Blackbeard said, letting Cooper down on his desk.

"What about the rats?"

"Let me worry about the rats. Ye need to get out there and help the rest of the crew. I want these captures to go smoothly."

Although he obviously didn't like his captain's response, Owen left anyway, slamming the door behind him. Blackbeard sighed as he rummaged through his chest for his pistols and the black flag. Meanwhile, Tuffy called Cooper over to where she was. Acting quickly, Cooper jumped off the desk and headed over to where Tuffy rested among the soft cloth.

"Cooper, you need to get down to the hold and take care of those rats right away," she said.

"But we had the rats under control," Cooper replied.

"I know we did, but things have obviously changed. If there is a rat situation down there, then they must have come aboard from the goods Blackbeard bought from Captain Ashworth and Captain Burgess. It's our duty to protect the ship, Cooper, and I'm counting on you to take care of this. I'm confident you will succeed."

"You can do it, Cooper," Marisol squawked from the desk chair.

"Just take those claws and scratch their eyes out," Marco added as he swooped through the air screeching as if he were fighting an invisible enemy.

The blue macaw's wild performance made Blackbeard look up. "What has gotten into ye, bird? First Cooper is acting like a scaredy-cat, and now ye are acting like ye swallowed a sack of sugar. I better have a talk with Stede."

Marco stopped flying around the room and rejoined Marisol on the chair. As Blackbeard returned to his chest of weapons, Tuffy again stated how much confidence she had in Cooper's ability to prove the pirates wrong. Cooper took a deep breath. He certainly didn't feel confident, but he couldn't say no to Tuffy. Being a ship's cat meant he would have to put his fears aside and handle the rats.

"Alright, Cooper, it's time for us to go back on deck," Blackbeard said as he walked to the door wearing his bandolier and flintlock pistols. "We both have a job to do."

Looking once more at Tuffy and his feathered friends, Cooper followed his captain out the door. By now, there was a lot of commotion on deck as the pirates prepared to take the prize ships. Quartermaster William Howard approached Captain Blackbeard almost immediately, leaving Cooper to fend for himself.

Knowing he had to face his fears, Cooper reluctantly went down the steps leading to the galley. He was halfway across the room when a familiar voice called out to him. It was Como.

"Hey, Coop! I was worried that Captain Blackbeard locked you up in a cage like he did me the other day."

"No, but I sort of wish he did. Owen told Blackbeard I was falling behind on my duties and deserved punishment. He even suggested to throw me overboard, although doing so would certainly bring bad luck to the ship," Cooper replied as Como hopped down from the table.

"Did he say what he thinks you did wrong?"

"He claims to have seen a bunch of rats down in the hold. Blackbeard told him he would handle it. I don't think Captain is mad at me, but I'm pretty sure he's disappointed."

"What are you going to do?" Como asked.

"I don't have much of a choice. Tuffy told me to take care of the situation, and Blackbeard said I had a job to do."

"Those rats are scary!"

"I know. The last thing I want to do is go down there by myself."

"I'll go with you, Coop. I can't help you kill them since I don't have claws and can't see well in the darkness, but I can at least sit on the stairs while you're down there so you won't be alone."

Touched by his friend's offer, Cooper tried to give him a smile. "Thanks, Como, you're a great friend."

With his little monkey friend by his side, Cooper trotted through the sleeping quarters. As they passed several hammocks of sick pirates, Cooper thought about the mission ahead of him. It was an important mission. One that would not only save the food supply, but also prove his loyalty and devotion to his job as a ship's cat.

Unfortunately, thinking about how proud Tuffy and Blackbeard would be didn't calm Cooper's nerves. In fact, his fear only got worse as he and Como descended the steps leading into the belly of the ship. Standing at the bottom of the stairs, Cooper allowed his green eyes time to adjust. He could hear scratching sounds coming from the opposite end of the ship's hull.

"Good luck, Coop," Como whispered as he nervously rubbed his long tail. "I'm afraid you're going to need it."

Leaving Como on the stairs, Cooper unsheathed his claws and headed into the darkness alone. Before long, he felt his fur brush against the ballast stones that kept the ship steady in the water. Staying in the center of the ship, he focused on the scratching sound. Every so often he paused to scent the air, hoping to pinpoint the enemy rats before they scented him. Cooper had almost made it to the front of the ship when the scratching suddenly stopped.

Fearful, Cooper tried not to panic as he carefully took a step backwards and prayed for the Mighty Creator to give him strength. His mind raced as he wondered if the rats had heard him or perhaps smelled his scent. He reminded himself that their eyesight was probably better than his since they spent all their time in the darkness.

As Cooper debated what he should do next, something jumped on his back. Now on the floor, Cooper let out a meow as the rat bit his right side. Cooper quickly turned over and scratched the creature with his back claws.

Pain radiated through Cooper's side as he stood up and faced his attacker. The creature staring back at him was the largest rat he had ever seen. It had filthy gray fur and a long, naked tail. When it hissed, Cooper could see its sharp teeth.

The rodent lunged at Cooper, but thankfully he was able to dodge the second attack. Keeping his focus completely on the rat, Cooper launched an attack of his own, pouncing on top of the gray creature with his claws. Furious, the rat hissed in protest as it tried to bite him again. The two opponents tussled with each other until at last Cooper was able to get a grip on his enemy.

Without hesitation, Cooper quickly bit the back of the rodent's neck, finishing him off. The rat gave one last shrill cry before going limp under Cooper's weight. Once he was sure his enemy had taken its last breath, Cooper cautiously stood up.

"Coop? Are you okay? I heard all the racket," Como hollered from the other end of the ship.

"I'm okay," Cooper yelled back, wondering if he really was.

His right side throbbed with pain from the rat bite, but at least he was alive. As he looked down at his dead opponent, Cooper remembered there were other rats waiting to attack. Owen had insinuated there was an infestation of them.

Knowing he needed to prove his dedication to his job, Cooper decided to take his kill upstairs to show Blackbeard and Tuffy. He could continue hunting rats later. Cooper bent down to grab the rat's gray fur in his teeth and started dragging it to the stairs. The task was difficult as he struggled to haul the heavy body past ballast stones and around the three giant masts that went up through the decks. Cooper had almost made it to the staircase where Como waited, when the ship suddenly lurched to one side with a loud boom.

Startled, Cooper dropped the limp rat's body and braced himself by digging his claws into the wooden hull beneath him. Another boom echoed through the ship accompanied by a second shift of the ship's weight.

"I think that's cannon fire, Coop. The *Queen Anne's Revenge* must be in battle," Como shouted from close by.

"I'm right here, Como, there's no need to yell," Cooper replied as he tugged on the rat a few more feet to the bottom of the stairs.

"Goodness, what a big rat!" Como exclaimed as Cooper dropped the creature on the last step. "Coop, you're bleeding."

The little spider monkey jumped down to Cooper's level so he could look at his bleeding side.

"It was a tough battle," Cooper replied.

"You better make yourself known to the pirate cook. He will care for your injury. Rat bites can easily make you sick. Just ask Rooney," a voice called out from under the stairs.

"Who's talking?" Como asked as he climbed up a few steps and peeped his head between the boards to see better.

"Why, it's me, Henrietta hen, that's who!"

"Just let those two go their own way, Etta."

"Why, I was just trying to help, Rooney. You don't have to be rude. Don't you want the young tiger to come back and save us from the horrible rodents?"

Como motioned for Cooper to join him. Leaving his kill behind, Cooper climbed up four or five steps and stuck his head between the boards like his friend was doing. Looking down, he found himself staring into the chicken cages tucked under the stairway. Two of the chickens were in separate cages. One had golden brown feathers while the other one, whom Cooper guessed was the rooster, had dark brown body feathers and magnificent, shiny-black tail feathers.

"Tiger?" Como gasped. "There's a tiger onboard?"

"Why, of course, dear. Isn't your friend a tiger?" Henrietta replied.

Cooper purred with laughter. No one had ever called him a tiger! Although he had never met one, he had seen a drawing of a tiger in one of the many books Como had shared with him in Stede Bonnet's collection. Como couldn't stop laughing either. The little monkey grabbed Cooper's tail as he playfully growled like a fierce tiger.

"I got you, Mr. Tiger, by the tail!" he laughed.

"That is no tiger, Etta, it is a ship's cat," Rooney the rooster said.

"Why, I do believe you may be right. I'm sorry I mistook you for a vicious beast, dear cat. You still need to have Cookie look after your injury, though. Why, it was only last year a really mean rodent attacked poor Rooney. Cookie saved his life," Henrietta added.

"I'll make sure to let Cookie know about it as soon as we find out what's going on," Cooper replied.

"Captain Blackbeard was preparing for battle when we came down here," Como explained.

"Why, mercy!" Henrietta gasped as she collapsed in her cage.

Rooney sighed and shook his beak, making the floppy red skin under his chin wobble. "Now, Etta, we've been through many battles. Captain Blackbeard has never lost yet." Then to Cooper and Como he added, "Don't pay any attention to her. She has this ridiculous idea that someday Blackbeard will lose the battle and the opposing crew will add us to their chicken stew."

Henrietta suddenly jumped up. "Why, Rooney, I'm ashamed of you! It is *not* a ridiculous idea. We really could end up in such a horrible situation."

"Sorry to interrupt, but we need to get back upstairs," Como said.

"Help me with this rat, Como, I want to show Blackbeard and Tuffy. We can leave it in the sleeping quarters while we find out what's going on," Cooper suggested.

"Okay, I'll pull on his tail while you push from behind."

The two friends worked together to get the dead rat up the stairs. It took a lot of effort, but at last they succeeded. Leaving the rat in the sleeping quarters, they scampered to the opposite end of the cabin and into the galley. Other than the handful of ailing pirates too sick to leave their hammocks, both rooms were empty.

Cooper got an eerie feeling as he crossed the wooden floor of the galley and followed his friend up the final flight of stairs to the top deck. He briefly wondered if the feeling was his own fear or the prickle he felt when something was going on. Hoping it was only his ship's cat instincts, Cooper stepped out on deck behind Como.

The air was thick with smoke, presumably from the cannon fire. A group of fifteen or twenty strangers stood in the center of the ship with three pirates guarding them at gunpoint. Captain Blackbeard was speaking roughly to one of the handsomely dressed prisoners while Captain Stede Bonnet looked on, rubbing his hands together nervously. Quartermaster William Howard stood near the captain's cabin with a pistol in hand, keeping an eye on the whole group.

"I beg you, sir, please let us go," the fancy man said to Blackbeard.

"Why should I?" Blackbeard countered sharply.

"Many of us are simply passengers on these ships. I happen to be on my way to London. We do not own the ships nor the contents of them, but I feel certain those who do will gladly give you all the contents in return for our lives."

Blackbeard laughed in such a way that made chills go down

Cooper's spine. "Ye think ye know what I want, but ye are wrong. I want more than the goods on these ships. I want all the jewels and money ye are carrying and then I want ye very lives."

The man's face turned so pale it matched his cream-colored stockings and fancy vest. "There are women onboard these ships, sir, and a least one child that I know of."

"So?"

"He's my son, sir, and only four years old. At least have mercy on his life and the lives of the fair ladies."

"Ye are in no position to demand mercy," Blackbeard replied, clearly enjoying the power he held over the captives.

"I am not demanding anything. You are obviously in control. I simply ask you to consider allowing them to live. There is no honor in murdering women and children."

Several of the women shrieked in horror and at least two of them fainted on the deck at his comment about murder. The other men and women around them quickly bent to see if they were all right.

Their actions didn't seem to affect Blackbeard. "Do ye think pirates have honor?"

"No, but—"

"But what? If we have no honor, then killing a group of prissy ladies and an annoying child is nothing to us."

To everyone's surprise, Stede Bonnet stepped forward. "Edward, I must ask ye to stop this nonsense. We can't murder these innocent people, especially the ladies and the poor child."

Blackbeard's cheeks grew red in his rage. Cooper folded down his ears, expecting him to unleash his fury on Stede, but he didn't.

"Where is this child?"

"Why?" asked the man, suddenly in a panic.

Blackbeard ignored him as he addressed his quartermaster. "William, locate the boy and bring him and his father to my cabin."

"Why do you want my son?" the man repeated as Blackbeard walked to his cabin and opened the door. When Blackbeard didn't respond the man added, "Did you hear me?"

Captain Blackbeard paused to look at the man. "I heard ye the first time. I need the boy."

Without another word, Blackbeard entered his cabin. Cooper and Como scurried in behind him. Tuffy immediately lifted her head to see what was going on as Blackbeard placed his three-cornered hat on his desk and sat down.

"What are you doing here, Cooper? I thought you were going hunting in the hold," Tuffy hinted.

"He did go hunting. Coop killed a huge rat!" Como exclaimed.

"Good for you. I knew you could do it," Tuffy said proudly. Then, seeing his injury she added, "My goodness, you're bleeding!"

Before Cooper could respond, William Howard came into the cabin dragging in the colonist while the newest member of the crew, John Martin, carried a little boy in his arms. The child was giving the pirate a hard time as he cried out for his father.

"What's going on?" Tuffy asked in alarm.

"Captain wanted to talk to this man privately. He and his son are passengers on one of the captured ships," Cooper explained as Blackbeard stood up.

Despite his own fear, the father gently reassured his young son that there was nothing to be afraid of. The boy stopped crying, allowing John Martin a chance to sit down with him in one of the straight-backed chairs in front of Blackbeard's desk.

"What are you going to do with us?" the colonist asked as William let go of his arm.

"Ye told me earlier when I was questioning each passenger that ye are a member of the council in Charles Town and are on ye way to London to meet with high-ranking officials. Right?"

"Yes."

"What is ye name?" Blackbeard continued.

"Samuel Wragg."

"And ye son?"

"His name is William, but we call him Will," Samuel answered.

"I assume ye own a great deal of land."

Samuel hesitated. "I do."

"And I presume ye have a close relationship with the governor?"

"Of course. What are you hinting at? Do you want more money?"

Again, Blackbeard laughed. "Why do men assume pirates only want money? Let me explain something to ye. I strategically anchored my fleet of ships across this sandbar in such a way that no ship can enter or leave the Charles Town port without passing us. Now, we have a boatload of hostages, many of whom are women. I also have a wealthy member of the council, who no doubt loves his son."

The councilman glanced at the blonde-haired four-year-old seated in John Martin's lap. Thankfully, the little boy had no idea what was going on as he playfully tugged on John's beard.

"Give me your demands. I will try to convince Governor Robert Johnson to give it to you. We should be able to row back to town in a day if you allow a few men to go with us."

"Us?" Blackbeard blurted out. "The boy isn't going anywhere.

Keeping him will guarantee that we get what we desire."

"I can't leave him here with you!" Samuel gasped.

"Perhaps ye should rethink this, Captain," John interrupted. "The boy is leverage to make sure his father returns, but will the governor grant our requests on the lives of a child and a few ladies? Holding the councilman hostage gives us a better chance of receiving our loot."

"I agree. Let's send someone else," William Howard added.

Blackbeard turned back to the councilman. "Is there anyone ye would suggest who has the governor's ear? Remember, ye son's life depends on ye honesty. I will not hesitate to kill ye."

"Yes, there are a couple of men who should have no trouble persuading Governor Johnson to fulfill your demands."

"Let's go talk to them. John, keep the lad in here," Captain Blackbeard ordered.

Samuel Wragg clearly didn't want to leave his young son alone with the pirate, but he didn't argue with Blackbeard. He simply told his son he had something he needed to do and would be back soon. Cooper watched as Blackbeard led the way out onto the deck with William and their prisoner behind him. Meanwhile, John Martin continued to play with the little boy. Surprisingly, the pirate seemed to be enjoying making the youngster laugh and clap his hands.

Seeing this other side of the pirate made Cooper wonder if Blackbeard had been bluffing when he claimed he would kill the poor boy as well as the other prisoners. Was it just a threat or something more? Cooper shivered as he considered what would happen if the pirates didn't get what they asked for.

 CHAPTER TEN 

Hostage Situation

Heavy drops of rain saturated every inch of the wooden deck as Cooper made his way to the bow of the ship. With his ears folded back and orange fur plastered to his body, he weaved in and out of tight places to keep from getting in the pirates' way. The crew had been working hard since dawn to get all the sails either taken down or tied off to avoid any damages in the wind.

By the time Cooper made it to the tiny wooden perch at the very front of *Queen Anne's Revenge*, he was miserable. Not wanting to stay any longer than he had to, Cooper quickly jumped up on the wooden board to have a look around. The iron chain connecting the *Queen* to the anchor tightened every minute or two as the ship rocked in the waves. Although the rain had made visibility difficult, Cooper could see the outlines of the *Revenge, Adventure,* and *Adventure II* anchored in a semi-circle on the same sandbar.

It had been several days since Blackbeard sent two pirates ashore with one of the prisoners named Mr. Marks. Blackbeard decided to keep the councilman, Samuel Wragg, and his son, Will, in case the first attempt to persuade the governor didn't work out. He also gave the two pirates a note addressed to Governor Johnson. The note demanded a chest of expensive medicine which the French doctor had suggested for the sick pirates.

Blackbeard gave the men a time frame to return to the *Queen*, but so far there was no sign of them. This worried Cooper. Did the governor decline Blackbeard's request or was something else going on? Cooper wasn't the only one concerned. Even Captain Blackbeard was on edge as the entire fleet waited to see what Governor Johnson would do.

Sighing, Cooper pounced onto the deck and made his way to the stern of the ship. He winced as the impact made his previously injured side ache a little. Thankfully, whatever Cookie had put on the rat bite had made the wound heal pretty well, but Cooper could still feel the injury whenever he jumped.

As Cooper walked swiftly past the pirates, he kept his ears tuned in to their conversations. Twice he paused to listen to the idle chit-chat among the members of the crew, but their conversations were only about the messy weather. Cooper was almost to the captain's cabin, when Cookie came up from the galley. To his surprise, the cook immediately pulled young JJ Brooks away from his work.

"JJ, I need to speak to ye father. Where is he?" Cookie asked.

"I don't know. What's wrong?"

"I'm afraid I can't tell ye, lad. Thanks anyway."

"Thomas Miller might know," JJ suggested as he pointed at the dark-haired pirate walking toward the captain's cabin. "Pa was helping him fold up some sails earlier."

"I should probably tell Thomas what's going on, too. I'll see ye later, lad," Cookie said as he ran to catch up with the pirate.

Curious to see what was going on, Cooper hurriedly followed the old pirate cook. He caught up with him just in time to hear part of his conversation with Thomas Miller.

"So, ye think he will actually do it?" Thomas asked.

"I don't know. He's acting strange. I haven't seen him this mad in quite a while," Cookie replied.

"What can Joseph and I do to help? I doubt Blackbeard will listen to us. We don't hold any rank."

"Joseph grew up with Edward near Charles Town so I figured he might have some sway. Blackbeard also respects ye and trusts ye judgment. If either of ye can just drag this thing out, then perhaps we can avoid a disaster," Cookie said.

Thomas rubbed his chin. "I guess we can try. Joseph went to check on Stede Bonnet in the captain's cabin. Stede was keeping an eye on the child today, but ye know how crazy he gets. Joseph thought it would be wise to make sure the two of them haven't gotten into any mischief."

"I hope Stede hasn't made a mess," Cookie said. "Blackbeard will sure enough be mad. I better get back to the galley and see what I can do to prevent a murder."

Cooper gasped as the two pirates split up, one going to the captain's cabin and the other down the stairs to the galley. Did he hear Cookie correctly? Was Blackbeard about to murder someone?

Deciding he better go find out. Cooper scurried down the stairs behind Cookie, glad to finally be out of the miserable rain. His stomach churned with fear and anxiety as he wondered who was going to be on the receiving end of Captain Blackbeard's wrath.

Was it one of the crew members? Several had made bold statements recently suggesting Blackbeard was no longer capable of serving as captain if he wasn't bold enough to take the town. Then again, perhaps it was one of the captives. Blackbeard did tell the hostage, Mr. Marks, that he would start killing the other prisoners if the governor didn't meet his demands.

As soon as Cooper's orange paws touched the floor of the galley, he could hear his captain's voice loudly accusing someone else in the room of meddling in his business. Not wanting anyone to spot him, Cooper quickly slipped under the table where he could safely watch Cookie as he attempted to reason with Captain Blackbeard.

"Edward, I'm not trying to meddle in ye business. We've been friends for many years. Now is not the time to ruin ye record. Ye have a legacy to uphold."

Blackbeard snickered. "A legacy? What good is a legacy unless ye are dead? Do ye know what they're planning to do, Cookie? They're planning to vote me out of my job. If I don't show leadership now, then my so-called legacy as a captain is over."

"I know there are quite a few men against ye on this, Edward, but that still doesn't give ye the right to ruin a life. Once ye turn to killing there is no going back. The truth is, I don't think ye have it in ye to kill the lad," Cookie replied.

"So, it's come to this? Even ye think I'm weak?"

"Nay, ye are the strongest person I know and a natural leader. But murder? It's not who ye are, Edward."

Before Blackbeard could respond, Joseph Brooks and Thomas Miller came down the stairs from the main deck, both soaking wet from the rain. From the look on Blackbeard's face, Cooper could tell he wasn't pleased to see them.

“I suppose the two of ye are here to talk sense into me as well. Did Cookie put ye up to this?” Blackbeard asked.

Joseph glanced at Cookie before answering. “Edward, we don’t want any more trouble than we already have. No one has the guts to challenge ye. There is nothing to prove.”

“I’m a man of principle. When I say something, I mean it. I warned the captives what would happen if we didn’t get the chest of medicine. Everyone heard it, including most of our crew. My patience was already running thin when the hostage and two pirates didn’t come back in two days like they promised,” Blackbeard said.

“They had a legitimate reason for passing the deadline,” Thomas spoke up.

“Ye mean that ridiculous story those fishermen told us?”

“Didn’t ye believe the fishermen? Why would they lie? They didn’t have to come tell us anything,” Cookie pointed out.

“I hope ye are right,” Blackbeard began, “but ye must admit the whole story about their rowboat capsizing in the stormy seas and them waiting on a sandbar for rescue was quite a tale. I really had no choice but to give them another chance. What am I supposed to do now? Their message said they hoped to arrive in Charles Town, see the governor, and get back here with the chest of medicine in a couple of days. That deadline passed the day before yesterday. I blamed it on the weather, but how can we be sure they even met with Governor Johnson? Perhaps they reached land and went their own way. Maybe the governor refused to comply with our demands or is planning an attack of his own.”

“Ye are right to question the motives of Governor Johnson, but surely the men would have enough sense to follow through with their mission to meet the governor. Both the captive ye selected and the two pirates from Israel Hands' crew on the *Adventure* knew how important it was to meet the governor as soon as possible," Joseph said.

"Aye, but did they?" Blackbeard asked.

The three pirates looked at each other, obviously not sure how to answer their captain. Cooper briefly wondered why they didn't seem to have confidence in their fellow crewmates who had gone ashore.

"It's time for me to do what I promised," Blackbeard continued as he headed for the stairs.

Cookie, Joseph, and Thomas all rushed for the doorway to follow their captain. In the chaos of their anxious voices, Cooper quickly left the safety of the table to keep up with them. A sickening feeling nearly overwhelmed Cooper's heart as he thought about what the fearsome pirate captain planned to do. He felt as though he should try to do something, but he didn't know what. Instinctively, Cooper started to pray. At this point only the Mighty Creator could change Blackbeard's heart.

By the time Cooper made it to the main deck, he had decided to talk to Tuffy as soon as he could get into the captain's cabin. Thankfully, the rain had let up some which was a good thing, but it didn't seem to bring any pleasure to Blackbeard. His attitude was just as gruff and mean-spirited as it had been down in the galley.

Without a word, Blackbeard entered his cabin with Cookie and Joseph while Thomas went to find the quartermaster, William Howard. Cooper managed to slip in between Cookie's feet, although the cook grumbled when he nearly tripped over him.

Once inside, Cooper darted for the corner of the room where Cookie had made the little bed for Tuffy. The solid black she-cat was meowing at Como who was doing flips on Blackbeard's desk. Meanwhile, Stede Bonnet was crawling around on his knees with the small child riding on his back. It reminded Cooper of his home in France where the humans often rode on horseback through the streets.

"What is going on in here?" Blackbeard yelled with his fists clenched and face turning the color of Marisol's scarlet feathers.

A panicked Stede Bonnet quickly slid the four-year-old Will off his back. "I-I was just trying to entertain the boy, Edward. We only wanted him to have some fun."

"Who is we?" Blackbeard questioned as he went to his desk.

"Me and my monkey, of course," Stede replied, getting up from the floor. "Will seems to enjoy animals. He likes the macaws as well, but he can't play with them."

"Ye weren't supposed to be playing with the boy. I told ye to just watch him," Blackbeard snapped.

"Nay, ye told me to keep the boy up here in ye cabin away from his father and the others. Ye were right to think about him. Poor lad didn't need to spend another minute in that darkness down in the hold. It's bad enough his father and the other hostages are down there in the damp, rat-infested hole of misery," Stede said.

"I didn't tell ye to play with him."

"Well, I assumed it didn't matter if I did. Children need attention, ye know."

"Let it go, Edward. The boy can't help what is happening. It isn't his fault we haven't received our loot. He didn't even make the choice to be on the ship we captured in the first place," Cookie spoke up.

Blackbeard sat down in the chair behind his desk as Como

jumped down, scattering a pile of papers on the floor as he went. Furious, Blackbeard shouted at the little spider monkey, but he wasn't successful in grabbing him as Como ran over to Cooper and Tuffy.

"Como, I told you to behave yourself!" Tuffy scolded him. "You know how upset Captain gets when you make a mess. How many times must I tell you to stop playing on his desk."

"I just wanted to make little Will laugh. I bet I'm the funniest monkey he's ever seen."

"You're probably the *only* monkey he's seen," Cooper pointed out.

Como grinned. "True, but he calls me 'kitty' so I must be the funniest cat he's ever met."

"It doesn't matter. I want to know about Captain. You came in with him, Cooper. Do you know what is bothering him? Is there a mutiny on our paws?" Tuffy wanted to know.

"A mutiny?" Como gasped as he held his tail tightly against his chest. "Are we seriously having to deal with a mutiny again?"

"Don't worry, the crew isn't planning to take the ship," Cooper said. "Blackbeard is upset about the missing men and the chest of medicine they are supposed to be returning with. He told Cookie and the others he had waited long enough. I overheard Cookie talking to Thomas Miller about him possibly murdering one of the hostages."

"Murder? I thought you told us Blackbeard had never killed anyone," Como replied, directing the last part to Tuffy.

"He hasn't killed anyone in the years I have served as his ship's cat. Now, that doesn't mean he hasn't severely injured captives who may have later died, or perhaps wished they had died. I haven't witnessed him injuring any captives, but I have seen it happen within his crew," Tuffy answered.

"So, what can we do?" Cooper asked.

Tuffy sighed as she glanced across the room at Blackbeard, who was lecturing Cookie, Joseph, and Stede on his determination to follow through with his promise by sundown. "I'm afraid there isn't much we can do. It sounds like Captain has spoken. All we can hope for is the swift return of those pirates and hostage before dark."

Cooper didn't particularly like Tuffy's response, but he didn't challenge her. Tuffy had been Blackbeard's trusted ship's cat for years. She knew him better than most.

A sudden entry into the cabin made everyone look. The new arrival was Quartermaster William Howard, who announced that there was an issue going on which required Captain Blackbeard's attention. Grumbling in frustration, Blackbeard got up from his seat, grabbed his tricorn hat from his desk, and left the cabin. Cookie and Joseph went with him to see what was going on, leaving Stede Bonnet alone with young Will and the animals. The gentleman pirate had just squatted on the floor to play with the child again when the door opened to the cabin revealing JJ Brooks.

"What are ye up to, JJ?" Stede asked the young pirate.

"Pa told me to come look after Will. Samuel Wragg is causing a ruckus below deck. He's upset about his son being up here and is demanding to see him."

"Well, now, I'll just take Will down there to him then," Stede said as he got up from the floor and grabbed the child's hand.

"Captain Blackbeard denied Wragg interaction with his son and refuses to allow us to break his orders. Cookie seems to think ye may be able to convince Wragg that his son is all right," JJ explained.

"I will certainly do my best to reassure him," Stede replied as he went to the little side room where he slept.

Bonnet returned to the main cabin a few moments later dressed in his fancy light gray coat. He put on his red-feathered, three-cornered hat, told JJ he had released the macaws so they could stretch their wings for a bit, and left the cabin with such a performance he acted as though he was the sole captain of *Queen Anne's Revenge.*

"I can't stand him!" Tuffy exclaimed as Stede slammed the door. "Bonnet thinks he's so high and mighty, but he's wrong. He owes Blackbeard big time. Bonnet wouldn't have any rank at all if it wasn't for Blackbeard saving his butt." Como snickered, causing Tuffy to narrow her single green eye in suspicion. "What are you laughing at?"

"I thought you were being funny by talking about Stede Bonnet's butt. Guess you didn't mean it as a joke," the little monkey said.

Tuffy didn't respond, but Cooper got the feeling she was annoyed with Como's antics. Her attitude didn't improve when Marco and Marisol flew into the cabin from Stede's sleeping quarters.

"Here comes those birds," Tuffy sighed as she laid her chin over her black paws.

Both macaws swooped through the air making Will giggle and clap in excitement. Laughing himself, JJ sat on the floor with the four-year-old. He pulled a small bag from his pocket. Thinking it was possibly Marisol's treasure, the animals got excited. Unfortunately, the thrill of seeing the clay flute again disappeared as JJ carefully poured out the contents of the bag, which revealed a handful of marbles.

"Sorry, Marisol," Cooper said to his feathered friend. "I was hoping he would pull out your flute."

"Oh, well, maybe we will figure out where he is keeping it at some point," Marisol replied as Como let out a shriek.

"Oh, boy! It's marbles," Como shouted enthusiastically.

Como immediately went over to JJ and the child so he could see the marbles better. The little monkey's squeals of happiness captured JJ's attention even if he couldn't understand what he was saying.

"Sounds like ye are an admirer of marbles, too, Mr. Monkey. Ye sure are a curious little critter. What do ye think, Cooper? Do ye like marbles?" JJ asked, turning to Cooper who was still sitting near Tuffy.

Cooper trotted over to JJ and tilted his head so JJ could rub him between his ears. After getting a good head rub, Cooper was pleased to get JJ to scratch his chest fur as well. This led to Will wanting to come over to pet him. Cooper remained as still as possible as the little boy roughly patted him on his head.

"Kitty nice," Will said as he looked up at JJ with wide eyes.

JJ chuckled. "Aye, Cooper is a nice cat. He likes it when ye pet him. Be gentle, though, or he might scratch ye."

While Will petted Cooper, Como played with the marbles, rolling them back and forth on the floor. Soon, Will wanted to play too, prompting JJ to spread the four-year-old's legs apart so the marbles stayed between them. With Como and Cooper batting the multi-colored marbles across the floor, the game proved to be fun for all. JJ seemed to be particularly surprised by Cooper and Como's interest in the game. Marisol and Marco sat nearby on the desk, squawking from time to time and occasionally ruffling their colorful feathers.

For about an hour or so, all was right with the world. Cooper was having so much fun he temporarily forgot about Blackbeard's plan to execute one or more of the hostages by sunset. He was so fascinated by the new game of batting marbles that he jumped when the cabin door opened suddenly. The new arrival was none other than Captain Blackbeard.

"JJ, take the boy out on deck," the tall, bearded captain ordered.

"Why?" JJ asked as he stood up.

"I just gave ye a direct order, JJ, and I expect ye to follow it."

JJ's cheeks flushed red as if he regretted challenging his captain. He quickly scooped up the marbles and dropped them back into the bag while Will tugged on his britches, whimpering. On the other side of the room, Blackbeard had unlocked the wooden chest behind his desk and was rummaging through it.

Curious, Cooper peeked his head around the edge of the desk just in time to see Blackbeard load a flintlock pistol with black powder and tuck it into his belt. Just the sight of the pistol caused Cooper's orange fur to bristle. Fear gripped his heart as he realized Blackbeard was preparing to commit murder. Not knowing what else to do, Cooper went back to his friends.

"I just saw Captain Blackbeard load a flintlock pistol. We need to follow him to see what's going to happen," Cooper said.

"Why would he need a gun?" Marco asked, fluttering his blue, yellow, and green feathers.

"He's going to kill one of the hostages," Cooper responded.

Marisol gasped as she lifted her red, yellow, and blue wings to her beak. "Surely not!"

"We better hurry. JJ and Will are already leaving, and Captain

Blackbeard is right behind them," Como warned.

Not wasting any time, Cooper and Como headed outside. Tuffy called out to them, but Cooper couldn't understand her as the door slammed shut. By now, the rain had stopped. The air smelled fresh. It was the sort of freshness Cooper would normally rejoice over, but not today. A darkness seemed to hang over the *Queen Anne's Revenge*. It wasn't the gray clouds overhead or the looming darkness of night on its way, it was something deeper, something cruel and evil.

A crowd of people had gathered on the main deck. At first Cooper thought it was just pirates, but he quickly realized the hostages were in the crowd, too. To Cooper's surprise, ten or twelve pirates had surrounded the hostages and were holding swords and guns to keep them together. Blackbeard was in the center of the deck with his own gun drawn.

"Listen up. The time has come for me to deliver on my promise. I told ye what the consequences would be if the man ye sent ashore failed to return. Ye chose who to send among the five men I selected. I have been very patient and have extended the deadline twice. There will not be a third extension of grace. Mr. Marks came highly recommended by Mr. Samuel Wragg, so if there is anyone to blame it would be him. With that being said, I have decided to kill one person an hour, starting with Mr. Wragg's son."

Terrified screams echoed through the gathered crowd as Samuel Wragg tried desperately to reach his son. Unfortunately, the row of armed pirates refused to let him break their barrier. JJ Brooks, who had been holding the child, looked reluctantly at his own father, Joseph, as if silently asking if he had to give the boy over to Blackbeard.

"Please, sir, I beg you. Let my son go. If you must kill someone, then kill me," Samuel Wragg pleaded as he knelt in front of the ring of armed pirates.

The pleas of the boy's father and the shrill cries of the women didn't seem to bother Blackbeard as he ordered JJ to put the child down. JJ tried to argue with him, but Blackbeard refused to listen. Even Cookie and Joseph tried to change his mind.

"Put the boy down!" Blackbeard shouted.

"Ye can't kill the boy," Stede objected as he grabbed Blackbeard's arm. "He's just an innocent child. We are more civil than this."

Blackbeard yanked his arm away from him. "Pirates are not civil."

Stede grabbed him again, this time collapsing to his knees. He completely lost all dignity as he began to wail. Blackbeard pushed him away.

"Let go of me! Ye are not acting like a respectable captain or even a grown man for that matter. I've had enough of these games. I *will* execute anyone who continues to stand in my way immediately after I'm finished with the child. Now, I'm going to say this once more. Put the child down."

Clearly emotional, JJ put the four-year-old down and walked away from the scene, pushing aside fellow crewmates as he made his way to the front of the ship. Meanwhile, Stede got up from the deck and ran to the captain's cabin, leaving the door cracked long enough for Tuffy to join them on deck.

Cooper's heart pounded in his chest as Tuffy asked Como what was going on. The little spider monkey filled her in on the details as Blackbeard led the child to the stairs which went up to the quarterdeck. No one stepped up to stop him.

"This is terrible," Como sobbed as he turned his back and covered his eyes with his furry hands. "I can't watch. Why won't somebody stop Captain Blackbeard? Are they all so afraid of him that they will allow such an awful thing to happen?"

Como's words struck Cooper's heart. Was he right? Were the pirates scared of Blackbeard? All the mean statements about Cooper being a bad omen came flooding back to him. He considered Como's comments about taking chances and Tuffy's advice to believe in himself. Tuffy had trusted him to take care of the rats in her absence and had taught him how to be a true ship's cat Blackbeard could count on. What would a true ship's cat do in this situation? Would a pirate cat be fearful or would he stand up for what was right? Was this one of those times when he needed to take a chance?

Confidence surged through Cooper as he forced his fear aside. He was a pirate cat and pirates didn't back down. Glancing at Tuffy and Como, Cooper darted forward just as Blackbeard took a few steps back and held up his flintlock pistol.

The yells of the hostages and begging of Samuel Wragg were deafening at this point, but Cooper was no longer paying attention. He quickly took his stance between little Will and the fearsome pirate, Captain Blackbeard.

With his back to his four-year-old friend, Cooper unsheathed his claws and let out the loudest hiss he could manage. Blackbeard wasn't impressed. In fact, Cooper's defiance made Blackbeard angrier.

"Get out of the way, or I'll shoot ye, too!" the captain yelled as he attempted to kick Cooper to the side.

Reacting quickly, Cooper lunged at his captain, sinking his claws into his pant leg. Blackbeard screamed in pain as Cooper tightened his grip and bit down hard. If Captain Blackbeard planned to kill him, then he would go down fighting.

For several minutes, the fearsome pirate captain and brave pirate cat fought each other. Cooper hung on for dear life while Blackbeard tried desperately to pull Cooper off his leg. Blackbeard ordered several members of his crew to help him, but none dared to take on the rogue cat. Tuffy and Como watched in shock at a distance. The one-eyed she-cat pleaded with Cooper to let go of Blackbeard's leg, but Cooper was determined to stop him. At some point during the struggle, Blackbeard dropped his flintlock pistol and was able to finally force Cooper to let him go.

Breathless, Cooper stood away from his captain, gasping for air while Cookie picked up the gun. Blackbeard cursed as he bent on one knee to inspect his bleeding leg.

"Captain! Captain! There's a boat headed our way," called a voice from up in the rigging.

Everyone looked up into the sails to see Nathaniel Jackson waving at them. The pirate was holding onto the mast with one arm as he looked through a spyglass with the other.

"Is it another prize ship?" Quartermaster William Howard asked.

"Nay. It's a much smaller boat. I can't see it clearly yet, but it may be our fellow comrades and that Mr. Marks," Nathaniel replied.

"What do ye want to do, Captain?" Cookie asked Blackbeard as he held the flintlock pistol.

Blackbeard wiped his bloody hand against his britches and stood to face his crew. "Move the hostages below deck and prepare the ship for visitors."

"What about the boy?" asked the pirate named Owen Roberts.

Cooper recognized him as the one who tried to get him thrown off the ship after the rat episode. Owen was also on Cookie's watch list. Cooper recalled hearing Cookie say that Owen was sneaky. Interestingly, Owen was a close friend of Israel Hands, which was why Blackbeard had kept him on the *Queen Anne's Revenge* instead of allowing him to serve under Israel's command of the *Adventure*.

"I'll deal with the boy," Blackbeard said.

"Are ye still going to kill him?" Owen persisted. "Or have ye lost the nerve?"

Blackbeard gritted his teeth. "It is no concern of ye what I decide to do. I suggest ye help take these hostages down into the hold before I lose my temper."

Several pirates rounded up the hostages and began to usher them to the stairs leading into the belly of the ship. Somehow, Samuel Wragg managed to break away from the group long enough to grab his son. The relieved councilman hugged his four-year-old boy tightly as Owen tried to stop him. Surprisingly, Blackbeard ordered Owen to stand down and gave Mr. Wragg a few moments with his boy before separating them once more.

Not sure what would happen to the boy now, Cooper instinctively stood protectively in front of him again while Owen forced Mr. Wragg to follow the other hostages. Como quickly joined Cooper, vowing to help him guard little Will. The little spider monkey congratulated Cooper on winning the battle. Tuffy wasn't as supportive of his attack on the captain, but she did admit she was proud of him for standing up to his fears and fighting for justice.

Thankfully, Blackbeard didn't seem as enthusiastic about killing Will. The tall pirate captain sat down on the steps leading up to the quarterdeck as Cookie came over to look at his injured leg.

"Let me see ye leg, Edward. Cooper sure gave ye quite a fight," Cookie muttered.

Blackbeard winced as Cookie pulled back the cloth pant leg to reveal the bloody flesh underneath. "Aye. He's a pest. I don't know what I'm going to do with him. Perhaps he is a bad omen."

"Have ye considered his bravery?" Cookie asked.

"His bravery?"

"Aye. It took a determined spirit to stand up to ye, Edward. Even us pirates didn't have the guts Cooper has. I must admit I didn't have much faith in him to begin with, but he has proven himself as a ship's cat and more importantly as a pirate cat."

Blackbeard looked at Cooper. Wanting to show his devotion to the crew, Cooper stood as tall as he could. Tuffy and Como did the same, although the little spider monkey looked sort of odd as he stood at attention with his furry chest poked out. Meanwhile, little Will grabbed both Cooper and Como around their necks and gave them a big hug.

"Kitties my friends," Will said.

Overwhelmed with happiness, Cooper noticed Cookie and Blackbeard were amazed by the little boy's comment. Before either could say anything, William Howard walked up.

"The hostages are back in the hold, Captain. I also have news on the approaching boat. We have confirmation from the crew of the *Adventure* that the boat is indeed our fellow comrades. There are two men in the boat and a large wooden box between them. Unless it is a trick, ye got what ye wanted."

"Thank ye, William," Blackbeard said. "Get word to the other ships in the fleet to send the boat our way, and prepare our crew to haul up the boat when it arrives."

"Aye, aye, Captain," William replied, leaving to give out orders to the rest of the pirate crew.

When he was gone, Blackbeard looked back at Cookie, who was now trying to clean up the blood. "Well, I suppose ye are going to lecture me on losing my head."

"Nay, I think ye suffered enough under Cooper's claws. Just be glad he stopped ye from doing something ye would've regretted. Killing sailors or pirates is one thing, but a child is different. I fear ye have too big of a burden on ye shoulders. I thought shrinking the fleet from seven hundred men down to four hundred would help, but maybe ye should look at other options."

Blackbeard didn't respond. Cooper thought about what Cookie was saying. What kind of burden was he talking about? Whatever it was, Cooper hoped Blackbeard resolved it soon.

 CHAPTER ELEVEN 

Blackbeard's Plan

A nice summer breeze blew tufts of Cooper's orange fur as he sat on the top step leading up to the quarterdeck of *Queen Anne's Revenge*. The sunshine felt good against his fur. It was a pleasant feeling that matched the warmth in his heart. Life had been pretty good in the last few days. In fact, things had almost gone back to the way it was before the blockade of the port at Charles Town.

Several things had changed since Cooper's brave stand against Captain Blackbeard. Not only were the circumstances onboard the ship different, but Cooper had changed himself.

As Cooper soaked up the sun, he thought about Captain Blackbeard. Things had been difficult for the captain. Thankfully, the small boat rowed by the two pirates did indeed have the requested chest of much needed medicine. Mr. Marks did not return with the pirates, but it didn't matter. By the time the crew hauled up the medicine chest onto the *Queen Anne's Revenge*, no one seemed to care.

After having the French doctor inspect the medicine chest, Blackbeard ordered his men to release the hostages. Some of the pirates on the other ships didn't particularly like this. They urged Blackbeard to hold the hostages longer and to send another captive ashore with new demands of more worthy loot. Blackbeard refused to do such, claiming he had to follow through with his promise to let them go.

Seeing little Will and his father leave the ship had been a bitter-sweet moment for Cooper and his friends. Cooper was so glad the councilman and his young son were finally able to return home, but at the same time it was sad to see the four-year-old leave. Will had brought such joy to the ship.

The hostages didn't waste any time leaving the pirates behind. After they were on their way to shore, Blackbeard commanded the four ships in the fleet to prepare to set sail once again. It didn't take long for the ships to haul up their massive anchors. They left the sandbar off the southern Carolina coast and set a course for the northern Carolina shores.

Blackbeard's command was a surprise to most of the pirates who evidently had other plans to seek treasure in the Caribbean. The captain was determined to go north, though, and since no one demanded to hold a vote against him, his decision was final.

In the days since, Cooper often wondered why Blackbeard was so unwavering in his decision to sail north. He had asked Tuffy about it, but she wasn't really interested in knowing the reason behind his choice. Her only concern was to get back to her duties as a ship's cat, which forced Cooper to spend much of his time with her below deck hunting rodents.

Today had started out the same way with Cooper helping Tuffy kill seven mice and three rats. Tuffy killed more of the rodents than Cooper did, but he was steadily improving his skills. He was even more successful at keeping his fear at bay. After the hunt and a brief check of the main deck, Tuffy followed Blackbeard into his cabin while Cooper made his way up to the quarterdeck where he could give his fur a good licking without getting in the pirates' way.

It wasn't long before Como joined Cooper. The little spider monkey had been up in the rigging for most of the morning, enjoying swinging from the ropes holding up the sails.

"What are you doing, Coop?" Como asked.

"Relaxing," Cooper answered.

"Relaxing? That's no fun. I wish you could learn how to climb and swing like I do. It's so much fun, Coop. You can see forever."

"I doubt I would like it," Cooper replied.

"If you did climb, then you would know how close we are to land."

"Land?" Cooper asked in surprise.

"You heard me right. We are nearing land. I think it's the mainland Captain Blackbeard talked about the other day."

A commotion down on the deck caused Cooper to sit up and Como to stop talking. The pirates seemed to be in a tizzy as one of them started to climb the main mast in the center of the deck. Cooper recognized the pirate as Nathaniel Jackson, who held the job of being the ship's lookout. The scrawny pirate looked like a monkey as he climbed the wooden pole.

When he was almost at the top, Nathaniel straddled the crossbar that held up the main sail and clutched the pole with his left arm. He took a spyglass from his pocket and held it up to his eye with his free hand. Cooper realized he must be looking at the mainland Como had just told him about.

"Land ho!" Nathaniel shouted.

A handful of pirates cheered as others shook their heads in disgust. Someone hurried off to tell the captain while several others went down to the galley to tell their crewmates. It wasn't long before the deck was swarming with pirates, all chatting and causing such a ruckus that Cooper couldn't make out what anyone was saying.

Suddenly, the group fell silent. Wondering what happened, Cooper realized Captain Blackbeard had just come out of his cabin with Tuffy and Stede Bonnet following close behind. Surprisingly, Stede was wearing brown britches and a tan shirt instead of the nightclothes he had been wearing for the last few days.

Captain Blackbeard walked across the deck to the main mast. He tilted his head up to the sky and asked Nathaniel what he saw from the rigging. Nathaniel quickly relayed information to his captain. It sounded like the scrawny pirate was giving Blackbeard an idea of how close the land was.

Once he had the information, Blackbeard told Nathaniel to come down. He then gave out instructions to other members of the crew and ordered his quartermaster, William Howard, to get word to the other three ships about the approaching mainland. Blackbeard motioned for Stede Bonnet to follow him as he climbed the stairs leading to the quarterdeck where Cooper and Como had been watching. Tuffy joined them as the three animals listened to what Blackbeard had to say.

Now away from the rest of the crew, Blackbeard spoke directly to his so-called co-captain. "Stede, I have an important job for ye."

The gentleman pirate nervously rubbed his hands together. "I-I'm not sure I can do it, Edward."

"Ye don't even know what it is yet," Blackbeard replied.

"Nay, but I haven't been well lately."

Blackbeard sighed. "Stede, I have told ye a million times it is all in ye head. We did what we had to do back at Charles Town. It is time for ye to shake whatever feelings of guilt ye have. The men look to ye as a leader. Ye need to get a grip and start acting like a captain. I have decided to return the *Revenge* to ye control."

Stede looked as if he would pass out. "What? I can't be captain again. The men hate me. There is no way they would vote me in as captain. Besides, I would rather be co-captain here on the *Queen Anne's Revenge* with ye."

"Why? So ye can wallow in ye misery? Ye have barely been outside since we left Charles Town, Stede. Don't worry about a vote, I'll make sure ye are captain. I'm doing this for ye own good, trust me."

Without another word, Blackbeard descended the stairs, leaving a very distraught Stede Bonnet behind. The pitiful gentleman pirate paced back and forth on the quarterdeck mumbling to himself and dabbing his forehead with a neckerchief. He then took off downstairs to the main deck and back to the captain's cabin where he had been spending so much of his time.

"What in the world is Captain Blackbeard thinking?" Cooper asked Tuffy. "Captain Bonnet isn't ready to lead a ship."

"Coop is right," Como agreed. "Stede is crazy. Just the other day he was still walking around in his nightclothes. Pirates don't wear nightclothes, and they certainly don't walk around outside with them on. He has always been a little nutty, but has really been acting strange since we left Charles Town. Stede isn't ready to be captain of a ship. I think he's sick."

"I don't believe he is sick, although he has lost his mind in my opinion," Tuffy responded. "Still, Captain Blackbeard thinks this is best. He has a plan. For his plan to work, Captain Bonnet will have to take control of the *Revenge*. The hardest part will be convincing the crew. Let's make our rounds, Cooper, to find out what the crew is saying about the mainland. Something tells me there are some pirates who don't want to make a stop."

"I can help listen, too. I'll go down to the galley and will catch up to you later," Como suggested.

The three friends hurried off to eavesdrop on the pirates. Once on the deck, Como went down to the galley while Cooper and Tuffy split up to cover the main deck. Cooper kept his ears tuned into the voices of the pirates as he weaved in and out of sails, crates, and feet. Most of the pirates were too busy working to be in conversation, but there were a few who were talking about the mainland and a place called Fish Town.

By the time Cooper and Tuffy made it to the back of the ship once more, Captain Blackbeard was telling his crew they should be at the inlet within the hour. Cookie was standing nearby, apparently waiting to talk to him.

"Garret told me ye wanted to see me, Captain," Cookie muttered, looking around to be sure no one was listening.

"Aye, I want to speak with ye in private. Is there anyone in the galley? Can we talk there?"

"Nay, there are too many going in and out. Why can't we talk in ye cabin?"

"Stede is in there again. I suppose we will just have to talk quietly here," Blackbeard suggested as he leaned his elbows against the railing of the ship in a casual manner.

Cookie did the same, acting as if it were the most natural thing in the world to be gazing out at the ocean while his fellow crewmates were busy working sails and rigging. Startled by this secretive conversation, Cooper glanced over at Tuffy, noticing she was surprised, too.

"What's going on, Edward? Is something wrong?" Cookie asked.

"It isn't anything we can't handle, Joseph," Blackbeard said. "I wanted to talk to ye first, but with all the commotion, I couldn't get word to ye without alerting the others. I've been meeting secretly with several of our closest friends all day. I spoke to Joseph Brooks first, then William Howard and Thomas Miller, John Martin of course, and Garret Gibbons. So far, all of them agree with me that the time has come to downsize the fleet."

Cookie glanced at him. "Downsize?"

"Aye. Ye know as well as I do, the fleet is getting too large to handle. They're beginning to get ideas about how things should be around here. Charles Town tested my power over these men, and I don't think I have the same control over them as I did a month ago. There is no doubt about it, there will be a mutiny unless I do something about it first, which is where my plan comes in."

"Alright, let's hear it," Cookie replied.

Blackbeard lowered his voice to a whisper. Cooper strained to hear what the tall, bearded captain was saying, but it was no use. He couldn't make out any of it. Cookie nodded occasionally until at last Blackbeard finished.

"What do ye think?" Blackbeard asked.

"Ye want my opinion?"

"Of course. We were friends long before we became pirates. I asked ye opinion two years ago, when we had to decide if we wanted to serve Queen Anne of England as privateers and later when Governor Eden wanted our help retrieving the gold coins from those shipwrecks. This decision will change our lives."

"Ye said the other fellows agree with ye?"

"Aye. It may be our only chance."

"Tell me what I need to do," Cookie said.

Blackbeard gave him a slap on the shoulder as the two friends discussed what role Cookie would play in the plan. Cooper listened, but what he heard didn't make any sense. Captain Blackbeard was asking Cookie to bring up the chickens and other supplies from down in the hold.

"Why does Captain want Cookie to bring the supplies up to the sleeping quarters?" Cooper asked Tuffy.

"It's part of his plan," she replied.

"Just what does he plan to do? Have you heard him explain how he intends to downsize a crew of nearly four hundred pirates?"

Tuffy hesitated. "No, I haven't heard the whole thing, but I trust Captain to do what is right for all of us."

Not wanting to be disrespectful, Cooper searched for the right words to say to Tuffy to show how concerned he was about this new plan; however, Como came up from the galley before he could think of something to say.

"There isn't much talking going on down below, at least not about Captain Blackbeard. Did either of you find out anything?" the little spider monkey asked.

Cooper shared what they had heard with his friend. When he finished, Como shook his furry head and announced that he was going to the captain's cabin to tell Marco and Marisol to prepare for some sort of plan to downsize the crew.

As the little spider monkey figured out a way to climb up high enough to open the door to the captain's cabin, Cooper felt a prickle go down his spine. The sensation caused him to shiver despite the warm summer day. His reaction got Tuffy's attention.

"What's wrong, Cooper?" she asked.

"Something isn't right. It's like you said awhile back, you can feel it in your bones."

Tuffy suddenly looked worried as she glanced over at Blackbeard with her single green eye. The tall pirate captain was now back on the quarterdeck with his wooden backstaff. Cooper remembered hearing how a sailor used the device to measure distance by holding the backstaff so it lined up with the horizon. It was much more accurate than the astrolabe, which required the sailor to stare into the bright sun.

"Are you sure you felt the warning prickle?" Tuffy asked. "I haven't felt anything, and I normally do when danger arises."

"I felt something, although I could be wrong."

"Let's take another sniff around the ship. I trained you well, Cooper. If you felt the warning then we must investigate. I will meet you at the bow."

Tuffy trotted down the right side of the ship. Cooper was about to start down the left side when Como returned from the captain's cabin. After giving the little monkey an explanation of what they planned to do, Como offered to go with him. The two friends scurried off, listening to the chatter among the pirates. Cooper stopped numerous times to scent the air, but all he could smell was sweat and the salty sea. Unfortunately, the closer to the bow they got, the more prickle feelings he had.

When they arrived at the bow, Tuffy was waiting for them. The frazzled she-cat sat on the wooden board reinforcing the front of the ship. Cooper shook his haunches and jumped up to join her while Como climbed up beside him.

"Do you still feel it, Cooper?" Tuffy asked.

"Yes, it's getting stronger. Don't you feel anything?"

"No, which bothers me. There isn't a gray cloud in the sky so I doubt a storm is coming. I just don't understand."

Cooper sniffed the air. This time, his nose picked up the smell of dirt among the usual ship smells. Thinking it might be helpful, he quickly relayed the information to Tuffy, who revealed she had detected the smell of land ahead as well. From this new vantage point, Cooper could see how close they were to the approaching land. A long island protected the mainland which was only a short distance beyond it.

"Ahoy! Can ye hear me?" called a voice from the back of the ship.

Turning to see who it was, Cooper realized the voice belonged to Captain Blackbeard. The tall, bearded pirate was standing on the quarterdeck of *Queen Anne's Revenge* holding his brass speaking trumpet used to communicate with the other three ships.

A pirate wearing a bright red shirt stood at the railing of the *Adventure* with his own speaking trumpet. Cooper recognized him as Israel Hands, the captain of the *Adventure*. Two other men stood at the railings of the *Revenge* and *Adventure II* waiting further instructions from Blackbeard.

"Aye, we can hear ye, Captain," Israel shouted back through his brass speaking trumpet.

"We are near enough to land to start lining up. I want the

Adventure to sail through the inlet first, followed by the *Adventure II* and *Revenge*. I will sail the *Queen* in last since she is the largest of the four ships," Blackbeard commanded.

"Shouldn't we wait for the tide to come in, Captain?" Israel asked. "The water may be too shallow to pass through the inlet safely. Ye do remember that the inlet here at Fish Town is tricky."

"I remember, which is why I'm sending the smaller ships in first. Just keep ye ships as close to the bank as ye can. If ye do, then we will all miss the sandbar and pass through fine. Also beware of other ships tucked on the sound side of the island. The last thing we need is a run-in with the Royal Navy. I doubt we will see them this far south of the inlet at Ocracoke, but ye can never be too careful."

The three captains nodded as they set to work getting their ships in order and following through with Blackbeard's orders to line up. Meanwhile, Tuffy, Cooper, and Como jumped down to the deck and made their way to back of the ship. They had just managed to weave their way to the captain's cabin door when Stede Bonnet popped out wearing his full pirate attire.

"Ye look a lot better," Blackbeard said as he walked up.

"I don't feel better. Did I hear ye correctly? Are we nearing Fish Town already?" the gentleman pirate wanted to know.

"Aye."

Stede straightened his long, light gray coat. "Then I shall be ready to go ashore to meet these fine people."

Blackbeard sighed as he rubbed his black beard. "Stede, we are not going ashore to meet people. Number one, we are pirates, not gentlemen who drink tea and chat about the latest crop reports. Number two, this is Fish Town. They are more like a tiny village

than a town and aren't even worth our effort to steal from. Charles Town was a major port. Bath is also a port, although they are small compared to Charles Town. There is one thing Bath does have. It is home to Governor Charles Eden."

"Bath is north of here, right?" Stede asked.

"Ye are correct. Take this spyglass, and keep an eye on the other ships for me. If any of them look to be in distress, let me know immediately."

"What will ye be doing?"

"What do ye think? Someone must steer the ship."

"Right. Very well then, I will do my best to do as ye asked."

Captain Bonnet marched up the stairs to the quarterdeck while Captain Blackbeard took his place behind the ship's wheel. There was so much commotion on deck it was hard for Cooper to keep up with. Pirates scurried across the deck moving sails and tying off ropes as they adjusted to the wind conditions and the commands of their captain. Numerous times, Cooper, Tuffy, and Como had to move out of the pirates' way.

In no time, word came from the other ships that the *Adventure* made it through the narrow inlet. News of its successful entry and the fact there were no other ships hidden behind the island made the pirates cheer. Their enthusiasm grew as news of the safe passage of both the *Adventure II* and the *Revenge* reached them. With all three ships through the inlet, everyone's attention turned to the *Queen Anne's Revenge.*

Blackbeard stood with both hands firmly gripping the ship's wheel. He occasionally moved the wheel slightly to one side and then the other as he navigated the inlet. Twice, the bearded captain told his men to change the position of a few sails which caused a flurry of movement as they carried out his orders.

Then it happened. Cooper wasn't sure who started yelling first, but suddenly there was a lot of chaos. Even Stede Bonnet was hollering. Irritated, Blackbeard put two fingers in his mouth and let out a long whistle. The pirates froze.

"What are all of ye gawking at?" Blackbeard shouted angrily.

"Ye are getting too close to the sandbar, Captain," one of the younger pirates replied.

"Are ye suggesting I don't know what I'm doing?"

"Nay, I wasn't suggesting anything, sir. Sorry if I offended ye," the young pirate muttered.

Out of the corner of his eye, Cooper noticed Cookie whispering something to John Martin. The next thing Cooper knew, John was walking up to Thomas Miller, who in turn passed the secret on to JJ and his father, Joseph Brooks. One by one, the five pirates silently went down to the galley. Their mysterious behavior made Cooper wonder if whatever they were doing had anything to do with Blackbeard's plan.

"Come on, let's go up to the quarterdeck with Captain Bonnet," Tuffy suggested. "We can see better from up there."

As Cooper followed Tuffy and Como up the stairs, he tried desperately to calm his nerves and his growing fear. He reminded himself that he was a brave pirate cat who had faced scary rats and had even stood up to Captain Blackbeard. Feeling a tad better, Cooper thought about all the things the Mighty Creator had gotten him through. Surely the Mighty Creator was still with them now.

Cooper was about halfway up the stairs when the whole ship

shook violently. Reacting on instinct, Cooper unsheathed his claws to keep his balance, but the impact was too great. He tumbled down the stairs and landed on the deck with a painful thud. Both Tuffy and Como landed beside him.

Stunned and sore, Cooper sat up. All around them pirates had either knelt on one knee or were flat on their backs. Several called out in pain as their fellow crewmates rushed over to help their injured comrades. Captain Stede Bonnet was the first to state the obvious.

"Edward, I think we ran aground," he called out from the quarterdeck as he scrambled to his feet.

"Don't be ridiculous! Of course, we ran aground. Ye don't have to be intelligent to know what just happened," the mean-spirited Owen Roberts snapped.

"There's no need for ye to be hostile. Edward wanted me to let him know if a ship was in distress. Well, our grand ship is currently in distress," Stede replied.

"I've heard enough of ye bickering," Blackbeard interrupted. "The wind must have changed on us at the last moment and sent us off course. Instead of fussing about what happened, we need to focus on getting the *Queen* off the sandbar. William, choose four or five men to go with ye by periauger to the *Adventure*. Tell Israel to ease the ship into the inlet and pull her around to the portside of the *Queen*. In the meantime, ye men can start moving everything to the starboard side of the ship. My plan is to grapple the ships together with our grappling irons. Hopefully, the *Adventure* will be able to come alongside the *Queen Anne's Revenge* and pull her off the sandbar with ease."

William immediately set to work, uncovering the periauger in the center of the ship and choosing four of his crewmates to go with him. As Cooper watched the pirates, he realized William seemed to already know what to do despite having listened to his captain. Thinking this was odd, Cooper came to a startling conclusion. Did William Howard know something that his fellow crewmates didn't?

Cooper's mind whirled with possibilities. The more he thought about the strange behavior of William and the five pirates who had mysteriously disappeared below deck, the more Cooper realized they seemed to be acting according to a previously determined outcome. Could it be they were enacting Blackbeard's plan? What did this plan consist of and what did Blackbeard wish to accomplish other than somehow downsizing the crew?

All these questions yearned for answers. Unfortunately, there was no time to run any of them by Tuffy as the pirates prepared to let down the periauger off the side of *Queen Anne's Revenge*. Once William and his comrades were in the water, they started to row out to meet the *Adventure*. Meanwhile, Blackbeard supervised the pirates as they worked to move everything from the left side of the ship to the right.

"Come along, Cooper. We need to go to the front of the ship again," Tuffy announced as she took off at a fast pace.

Trying to keep up with her, Cooper did his best to avoid the working pirates. Como followed them to the front of the ship and joined him and Tuffy up on the ledge. From up here, Cooper noticed the periauger of pirates had gotten the attention of the *Adventure*'s crew and were now rowing back to the *Queen*.

It didn't take long for the crew of the *Adventure* to reverse their sails and start making their way back into the channel. The closer

it got to the *Queen*, the busier the pirates on either ship became. Between the two ships, over a hundred pirates were actively trying to prepare to grapple them together without bumping into each other.

Cooper watched and waited, hoping all would go well and knowing disaster could strike at any moment. A thousand things could go wrong, but with the *Queen* stuck on the sand beneath her, there weren't many other options. If they didn't get her off the sandbar soon, the ocean waves would eventually cause damage to her hull.

Time seemed to stand still as the *Adventure* crept closer to the *Queen Anne's Revenge*. Cooper could now see the pirates on the *Adventure* clearly. He also spotted Prissy standing guard on her ship's bow, surveying the scene just like they were. In the background, Cooper could see the *Revenge* and *Adventure II* anchored a short distance away with their own pirate crews looking on with anticipation. The silhouettes of Gunner and Blaze stood on their bows.

"I see your ship got stuck," Prissy shouted from her perch.

"Yes, we seem to need a little help," Tuffy yelled back. "Captain Blackbeard plans to grapple our ships together. He thinks with a yank from the *Adventure*, we will be able to float off this sandbar. You may want to brace yourself."

"I will. You should probably do the same," the black and white she-cat said as she suddenly lurched backward.

Prissy clawed her way back up to her post while Cooper, Como, and Tuffy watched in shock. Concerned and feeling helpless, the three of them could do nothing as Prissy struggled to keep her balance. The *Adventure* shuddered to a complete stop only a few yards from the *Queen*. In fact, with a running start, Prissy could have probably jumped aboard the *Queen Anne's Revenge* if she tried.

"What in the world happened?" Prissy exclaimed in surprise.

"I think your ship has run aground, too," Tuffy replied.

Sure enough, Tuffy was right. Many of the pirates cursed as they leaned over the sides of their ships analyzing the situation. To Cooper's amazement, Captain Blackbeard arrived at the bow of *Queen Anne's Revenge* to get a better look at the condition of the *Adventure*, which now had an enormous hole in the bottom of her hull. The tall, bearded captain pushed Cooper aside with his left arm as he leaned over the railing to look at the ocean and sandbar down below. Israel Hands appeared on the *Adventure*'s railing with a worried look on his face.

"Captain, I don't know what happened. The men did everything right," he said.

Surprisingly, Blackbeard seemed calm despite the dire circumstances. "Ye tried. We'll just have to look at other options."

"What other option do we have, Captain? Should we send word to the crew of the *Revenge* to start sailing this way? Perhaps they can pull at least one of us off the sandbar."

"I have another idea. Do ye still have the winch on ye ship or was it moved to the *Adventure II*?" Blackbeard wanted to know.

"Aye. It's here on deck. Why?"

"Lower it into William's periauger," Blackbeard ordered.

The pirate captain then waved his hand to get William's attention below him. When the quartermaster had signaled that he was listening, Blackbeard gave him and the four pirates in his company instructions to get the anchor winch from Israel's crew and to be ready to accept an anchor from the *Queen Anne's Revenge*. He then laid out plans for them to row the periauger into the channel, drop it into deeper water, and use the anchor winch to try dragging the ship off the sandbar inch by inch. The plan seemed crazy, yet no one offered any other suggestions.

Once the pirates started following his orders, Blackbeard looked down at Tuffy as he ran a rough, wind-chapped hand over her ears and down her back all the way to the tip of her tail. "Alright, Tuffy, we have work to do. Time to get part two of my plan rolling. Let's hope this goes smoothly. Keep ye eye on the men."

Blackbeard walked away, leaving Cooper feeling stunned. His instincts had been on point. Not only had the *Queen Anne's Revenge* run aground, but apparently, Blackbeard had steered the ship against the sandbar on purpose.

All Cooper could think about was why Captain Blackbeard would do such a thing. Wasn't *Queen Anne's Revenge* famous for being a fast ship for her large size? Why would Blackbeard want to deliberately damage her? The pirates had even called the grand ship Blackbeard's *Queen*. Didn't that mean he treasured her and treated her like the grand lady she was? What reason did he have for steering her too close to the sandbar knowing she could easily get stranded? Nothing made any sense to Cooper, but he knew whatever was going on wasn't over yet. This was only the beginning.

 CHAPTER TWELVE 

Watery Grave

Morning came as it always did, bringing bright beams of sunlight over the Atlantic Ocean's eastern horizon. This was no ordinary morning though. There was an odd feeling in the air. Cooper hadn't slept. He wasn't alone. Como, Tuffy, and the macaws had been wide-awake throughout the night too, all anxiously awaiting Blackbeard's next move. The pirates worked well into the night, doing what they could to preserve the *Queen Anne's Revenge* and the *Adventure*. Their efforts were admirable, but in the end, nothing could save the ships from a watery grave.

It was a gut-wrenching scene at daybreak when Captain Blackbeard addressed the crew of the *Queen Anne's Revenge* and the other three ships from his brass speaking trumpet. No one spoke as Blackbeard solemnly confirmed what they all knew was coming. Since neither ship was salvageable, the mission switched from attempting to get the *Queen* and the *Adventure* off the sandbar, to evacuating the ships altogether. With the *Revenge* and *Adventure II* already at full capacity, Blackbeard suggested they move the supplies to the island.

Cooper had overheard Cookie talking about the island, which the pirate called Bogue Banks. It was a deserted island, but still

within rowing distance from the mainland and the tiny village of Fish Town. Bogue Banks was a perfect place for ships to anchor and use while they careened the bottoms of their ships. The sound side of the island made it much easier for sailors to scrape, repair, and tar their ships without worrying about the ocean waves complicating things. As it turned out, it was also a perfect place for Blackbeard to use for the second portion of his mysterious plan.

For the most part, Blackbeard had succeeded in hiding his true intentions, even from Cooper and his friends. There were only a few times where the tall pirate captain slipped up when talking privately to the handful of pirates closest to him. In those rare moments, Cooper had strained to hear every word they were saying in hopes to better understand and perhaps brace himself for what was coming.

Unfortunately, there wasn't much to go on which left Cooper feeling helpless. Tuffy had been on edge, too. The she-cat had spent the entire night pacing the deck from the bow to the stern.

Now that it was dawn, Tuffy and Cooper made their rounds for what seemed like the hundredth time. Pausing to sniff the air, Cooper found himself yelled at by two irritated and sleep-deprived pirates who were carrying a crate between them. Scurrying out of the way, Cooper sighed with relief as he finally made it to the front.

"What took you so long?" Tuffy asked him from her perch on the board reinforcing the front of the ship.

With a shake of his tail, Cooper jumped up beside her. "I had a few obstacles to go around."

"Well, it appears the pirates have finished emptying the *Adventure*'s hold which means they will soon be over here helping our crew finish hauling everything to shore. Have you heard anything unusual from the crew?" Tuffy wanted to know.

"Just a bunch of grumbling. What about you?" Cooper replied.

"Like you said, nothing important. Let's go back to the quarterdeck and see if the monkey has any new information."

Cooper joined Tuffy as the she-cat retraced her steps to the stern of the ship. In no time, they were climbing the stairs leading up to the quarterdeck where they had last seen Como. To their surprise, the little spider monkey wasn't the only one on the quarterdeck. Both Captain Blackbeard and Captain Bonnet were there as well.

"Edward, I need to speak with ye in private," Stede said.

Blackbeard lowered the spyglass he had been using. "Now?"

"Aye, it is important."

"Alright then. Come with me to my cabin."

The two pirate captains descended the stairs. Tuffy took off after them with Cooper and Como right behind her. Luckily, all three animals managed to slip through the doorway just as it was closing.

As Cooper's green eyes adjusted to the dim light, he noticed Blackbeard was sitting at his desk while a very distraught Stede Bonnet stood facing him. The gentleman pirate spoke in a nervous tone as if he wasn't sure how to say something. Marisol and Marco watched from a straight-backed chair in the corner.

"Edward, I have done some serious thinking since last night," Stede began. "We are in a dangerous situation. It looks like the *Queen Anne's Revenge* will be a total loss, but it may take a while for the waves to overwhelm the ship."

"What's ye point?" Blackbeard interrupted.

"We are vulnerable!" Stede exploded. "Right now, we are like ducks swimming on a pond not realizing hunters are hiding in the bushes ready to shoot us and eat us for Sunday dinner."

Cooper widened his eyes in surprise. The gentleman pirate was hysterical as he talked and paced the cabin. Blackbeard sat emotionless behind his desk, occasionally stroking his beard. After a while, Stede stopped pacing.

"Are ye finished?" Blackbeard asked.

"Don't ye understand? If the Royal Navy spots us, we will be in serious trouble. We might even hang."

"Stede, I'm doing all I can to get our supplies to shore. There is nothing else we can do. Unless . . ."

"Unless what?" Stede asked.

Blackbeard leaned forward and propped his elbows up on the desk. "Never mind. I couldn't ask ye to do such a favor for me."

"Would it save us from the Royal Navy?"

"Maybe, but it would be a dangerous journey."

"Tell me what ye have in mind."

"Someone needs to sail up to Bath and meet with Governor Charles Eden," Blackbeard said. "We need to throw ourselves at the mercy of the governor and request a royal pardon. If we each had a paper pardoning us from piracy, then we wouldn't worry about the Royal Navy capturing us or taking us back to Virginia to hang."

"I can do that," Stede suggested. "Just give me a periauger and a few men. We can row up the shoreline and across the sound to Bath. It shouldn't take long, a day or two at the most. I will personally meet with Governor Eden, explain our circumstances, and get the pardons. Ye can count on me, Edward. I won't let ye down."

"I never doubted ye, Stede. Let me get some gold dust from the communal plunder. A sack of gold dust might come in handy when ye are negotiating with Governor Eden for those pardons."

Cooper watched as Blackbeard walked over to the wooden chest behind his desk. The pirate captain slipped a key from his pocket and used it to unlock the chest. Blackbeard pulled out a cream-colored sack, presumably filled with gold dust. He then locked the chest back and brought the sack to Stede.

"This should be enough to catch Governor Eden's attention. Tell him the rest of us can come in small groups to get our pardons if he needs to witness us signing our names to the document. Charles Eden is a reasonable man, at least he was the last time I saw him. Ye shouldn't have any trouble if ye tell him ye have been sailing with me," Blackbeard said.

Stede looked surprised as he took the sack of gold. "I didn't realize ye had met Governor Eden. How well do ye know him?"

"We've shared a few bottles of peach brandy over the years. Anyway, ye should get going. If ye leave right now ye might make it to Bath by midnight."

"Ye have a point. Let me get my coat and hat," Stede replied as he hurried off to his room.

Stede returned wearing his long, light gray coat. He quickly added his black, three-cornered hat with the bright red feather as he picked up the sack of gold he left on Blackbeard's desk.

Suddenly, the ship shifted to the left side. Both Blackbeard and Stede grabbed the desk as Cooper crouched down, wondering what happened. Tuffy and Como did the same while Marco and Marisol let go of the chair they were perching on before it fell to the floor.

"Don't tell me we're sinking already!" Stede gasped.

"Calm down. We may be getting closer to sinking, but it will be a while before we are underwater. Let's go see what's happening," Blackbeard suggested.

Captain Blackbeard led the way out the door with Stede and the animals following close behind. The scene outside was a bit chaotic. Pirates swarmed the slanted deck, doing all they could to drag crates and barrels to the opposite side of the ship in hopes to balance the ship out. Their efforts didn't seem to be helping much.

Cooper unsheathed his claws to help keep his balance. It was hard to stand straight with the deck tilted to the left, but at least he had his claws. Como really struggled to keep himself upright.

"What's going on, William?" Blackbeard asked his quartermaster who had just walked up to them.

"Those powerful waves finally knocked the *Queen* over on her side, Captain. Luckily, we moved most of the supplies ashore. The *Adventure* is already on her side completely. Her crew is working to salvage the sails, rigging, and whatever boards they can. Looks like we'll salvage most of the ship even if it is in pieces. At least we can use it for repairs. I doubt we can save any of the *Queen*," William Howard said.

"Just keep at it," Blackbeard replied. "Look, there's something ye need to know. Stede has offered to sail up to Bath to meet with Governor Eden about getting pardons."

"I just need a few men to go with me," Stede added.

"I'll get a group of men together and have one of the periaugers ready for ye," William said.

It didn't take long for William to choose several pirates to go with Stede. In fact, it seemed like he already had an idea of who to pick since he singled out specific men. Meanwhile, Cookie brought up a small barrel of rum and two large sacks of food for their journey.

As Cooper witnessed all this, he realized no one had told Cookie about the trip to Bath and yet the pirate cook knew exactly how much provisions they would need. Could it be that the decision to go up to Bath to meet Governor Eden hadn't been Stede's idea to start with? Did this have anything to do with Blackbeard's mysterious plan?

Surprisingly, the crew of the *Queen Anne's Revenge* didn't question the timing of Stede's sudden trip to the colony's main port at Bath. They were too preoccupied with lowering the remaining supplies from the *Queen* to the waiting periaugers. By the time Stede's small crew was ready to disembark on their journey north, the other pirates were hauling Cookie's big, iron cauldron up the stairs from the galley. While they dragged the heavy cauldron across the slanted deck, William Howard approached Stede, letting him know the periauger was ready.

"Thank ye, William. I do have a few orders to give out before I leave. Have ye seen young JJ Brooks?" Stede asked.

William exchanged a worried look with Blackbeard and Cookie, who lingered to see Stede off. "Nay. Is there something I can do?"

"I just need to give JJ some instructions," Stede replied.

"Instructions?" Blackbeard blurted out. "Stede, ye need to get going. Whatever ye had in mind for JJ will have to wait."

"But it can't wait!" Stede exclaimed.

Blackbeard's face turned red. Cooper braced himself for an angry outburst, but Blackbeard managed to speak without yelling.

"If ye don't hurry—" Blackbeard began through clenched teeth as a stream of pirates came up from the galley carrying cooking supplies.

"There he is," Stede said. "Come over here, JJ. There is something I need ye to do."

Startled, JJ left the line of pirates to see what he wanted. He glanced at Captain Blackbeard as if silently asking what was going on.

"I will be gone for a couple of days on official business," Stede said. "I am assigning ye the duty of looking after my exotic animals. This ship is sinking fast so ye will need to put them in crates and send them ashore. Also, be sure to box up my book collection and don't let them get wet. That is all, ye can go back to ye duties."

JJ gave the gentleman pirate a nod of understanding before walking away with his basket of bowls, plates, and pewter cups. Satisfied, Stede said farewell to Blackbeard, Cookie, and William as he swung his leg over the side of the railing and climbed down the rope ladder to the waiting periauger. As soon as he sat down, the group of pirates already in the boat started rowing away from the *Queen Anne's Revenge.*

"I didn't think he was ever going to leave," Cookie said.

"I'm surprised he's going at all. How did ye convince him to leave, Captain? Did ye have to threaten him?" William asked.

"I simply dropped hints about Bath and Governor Eden. Then I pretended we needed someone to go meet with Eden on our behalf. Stede took the bait like a hungry fish. The next thing I knew Stede was volunteering to go to Bath," Blackbeard explained.

"Do ye think he'll actually meet with the governor?" Cookie asked.

"He may be fearful of meeting with him, but he's more afraid of hanging. Getting a pardon is the only way to save his neck from the gallows. Stede will do anything to get a pardon," Blackbeard replied.

"I hope it takes longer than two days. We need all the time we can get to pull this thing off. Maybe he won't come back," William said.

Blackbeard sighed. "Don't get ye hopes up, he'll be back. He left his exotic animals here, remember? Anyway, with Stede gone, we must work fast. How close are we to emptying the *Queen*'s hold?"

"The men should finish mid-afternoon," William told him.

Blackbeard shook his head. "We can't wait until this afternoon to enact part three of my plan. I'll give ye an hour to finish getting the supplies relocated."

"An hour!" William exclaimed. "There is no way. I have pushed the crew nonstop for the last twenty hours. It's been all-hands-on-deck with barely any breaks for water, food, or a quick trip to the head. At some point they are going to snap, and when they do, we'll be in a heap of trouble."

"We don't have a choice. Besides, their exhaustion will work to our advantage. Just get the important stuff off the ship and leave whatever else behind," Blackbeard instructed.

"Should we leave Stede's books?" Cookie asked.

"Nay, pack them up. But put them on the periauger going to the island, not the one stocking the *Adventure II*."

"The *Adventure II*?" Cookie blurted out in surprise.

"I told William at daybreak to start taking all the important stuff to the *Adventure II* so we'll be prepared," Blackbeard explained.

Cookie rubbed his chin. "An hour will go by fast. I'll alert the others to the time change, Captain, and will get a few men to help pack up ye personal things as well as Stede's."

The three pirates split up, leaving Cooper alone with Como and

Tuffy. Cooper tried to process all he had just heard. His fur bristled with anxiousness, yet he wasn't scared.

"What do you think will happen to us, Tuffy?" Como asked.

Tuffy sat with her tail draped over her paws. She thumped the tip of her tail against the deck as she thought about the spider monkey's question. Always the impatient one, Como didn't wait for her answer.

"Captain Bonnet told JJ to take us to the island, but what if he doesn't? Surely, the pirates won't leave us on the *Queen Anne's Revenge* to drown," Como said. "I never got the hang of swimming. I mean, I could probably swim if I had to. You know, in a life-or-death situation. Of course, I suppose this *is* a life-or-death situation."

Tuffy narrowed her single green eye, indicating her annoyance with him. "Stop rambling. Captain Blackbeard won't leave us on the *Queen* to drown."

"Easy for you to say, you're his favorite," Como replied.

"Just do as you're told. Don't aggravate the crew. Don't try any pranks or act foolish up in the rigging. Don't do anything to make them mad. Most importantly, when the time comes to get into a crate, go peacefully with no attitude," Tuffy warned.

Como opened his mouth, but Cooper stopped him from talking with a flick of his orange tail. Cooper could tell Tuffy was in no mood to argue and besides, she had a good point.

"We'll do whatever you and Captain think is best," Cooper said.

"Good," Tuffy replied. "Cooper, come with me down to the hold to make sure everything is going well with the transfer of supplies. Como, go tell the macaws to be ready to leave the ship. Cookie and the others should be in there soon to start packing."

Cooper followed the one-eyed cat down to the galley. It was

difficult to descend the stairs with them leaning to one side like the rest of the ship, but Cooper managed to keep up with the older she-cat. They were almost at the bottom of the stairs when Cooper heard a commotion of clucks. Entering the room, Cooper spotted four dark-skinned pirates carrying the chicken cages across the threshold between the sleeping quarters and the galley. Henrietta, Rooney, and their feathered friends caused such a racket Cooper wanted to cover his ears.

"Henrietta's worst nightmare is coming true," Rooney said when he saw Tuffy and Cooper.

"Why, we're headed to the cooking pot for sure!" Henrietta added hysterically. "Please, dear cats, I beg you, please save us!"

"Stay calm, you'll be fine. Blackbeard ordered the pirates to move us to safety since the ship is sinking," Tuffy assured them.

Despite her encouragement, the chickens didn't seem to believe her. Cooper couldn't blame them. The whole situation was enough to make anyone panic. Unfortunately, Cooper didn't have time to panic, or to think about any bad things really. If he was going to survive, he had to think straight, trust Tuffy, and keep believing that the Mighty Creator was looking out for him and his friends.

Leaving the pirates to the task of forcing the chicken cages up the leaning stairs, Cooper followed Tuffy into the sleeping quarters. Several pirates took down the rows of hammocks while others stuffed loose clothing in crates for travel. No one seemed to notice two cats trotting swiftly to the other end of the room.

Once they reached the stairs leading to the belly of the ship, Tuffy changed her pace. To Cooper's surprise, the she-cat carefully eased down each step. Cooper understood why she needed to be cautious because of the leaning ship, but she hadn't acted this way on the other flight of steps. Oddly, Tuffy stopped suddenly about halfway down.

"What's wrong?" Cooper asked.

"Listen."

Cooper focused on his surroundings. He couldn't see far in the darkness, but he did hear something familiar, yet strange at the same time. After concentrating, Cooper realized it was the sound of water slapping the outside hull of the ship, except this sounded closer as if it came from inside. Confused, Cooper told Tuffy what he heard.

"You're right, Cooper. Let's go down a bit further."

Tuffy took a few more cautious steps down the staircase. Cooper did the same, staying right beside her. He stretched out his paw to go down a third step when he suddenly retracted it. Was he losing his mind? His paw felt wet. Deciding to try once more, Cooper extended his paw and discovered he wasn't imagining things. There *was* water just below him. A *lot* of water.

"How did all this water get down here?" Cooper asked.

"There must be a big hole in the side of the ship somewhere. The water is rising fast. No wonder the pirates got the chickens out."

Just then, Cooper heard voices above him. Looking up, he spotted the ship's gunner, Philip Morton, and the boatswain, Garret Gibbons, standing at the top of the stairs holding lanterns.

"We're too late," Philip grumbled. "There is no way we can get to those extra cannons now. Even if we did manage to find them, they probably wouldn't fire with all this seawater. If I had only thought about the cannons sooner, then we could've saved them all."

"Ye aren't to blame, Philip. The crew was focusing on getting the

Queen Anne's Revenge off the sandbar, not salvaging her cargo. It's a shame we lost several cannons, but we did haul right many of them out of here. The main thing is, we have plenty of cannons for the *Adventure II*. It's such a small ship compared to the gigantic *Queen*. She can't hold but so many cannons to start with," Garret replied.

Philip sighed. "Guess ye are right."

"We better get back on deck before Blackbeard makes his next move. It has almost been an hour since Cookie gave us the warning. There's no telling what will happen when the others discover we've tricked them," Garret continued.

The two pirates left the stairway, leaving Cooper alone again with Tuffy. Cooper's mind whirled as he pondered Garret's words. What kind of trick was Garret talking about?

"Let's go, Cooper. We can't do anything else down here. The rats are hopefully drowning," Tuffy said, climbing the stairs.

Cooper carefully climbed each step behind her, not wanting to accidentally slip and fall into the water down below. Once in the sleeping quarters, the two cats scurried past a few lingering pirates and followed Philip and Garret into the galley.

The nearly empty ship gave Cooper the creeps. It was an eerie feeling that reminded him of spooky places and scary ghost stories. Cooper also felt a sense of sadness as he walked one last time through the grand *Queen*. This wasn't just a pirate ship. The *Queen Anne's Revenge* was *his* ship. He had been her mouser from the start, and although he hadn't been the only ship's cat to serve on her enormous decks, he had been a big part of her journey.

Soon Cooper could see sunlight filtering down from the main deck. Sounds of commotion echoed above him. As Cooper set his orange paws on the top deck, he immediately spotted his little monkey friend who seemed relieved to see him and Tuffy.

"I sure am glad to see you! It has been crazy up here. You won't believe what the pirates are doing," Como exclaimed as he fumbled with a little cream-colored bag in his furry hands.

"What are you holding?" Tuffy asked.

"This is what I keep my treasures in," Como said as he pulled out several items to show them. "I have my lucky coin, a marble, a shiny button, and a few pages from one of Stede's books. Awhile back, I saw two pirates ripping out the pages and stuffing them into a cannon so they could light it. I kept what they didn't use."

A loud squawk grabbed Cooper's attention. Looking toward the front of the ship, he noticed several pirates tying a rope to the top of a cage. The cage had something colorful in it.

"Poor Marco and Marisol," Como said. "JJ and Cookie wrestled them into a cage a little while ago. They are fixing to drop their cage into a periauger now. I just hope the pirates don't start killing."

"Killing?" Cooper gasped. "What are you talking about?"

"Didn't I tell you, Coop?" Como replied. "The pirates got out their weapons, or at least some of them did. They're preparing a takeover. A mutiny. A rebellion."

"We get the idea," Tuffy interrupted him. "There is no need to panic. Captain Blackbeard has everything under control."

"I should say so! He's the one leading the mutiny," Como added.

Before Cooper could respond, Captain Blackbeard walked up. The tall, bearded captain now wore a sword at his side and two flintlock pistols in his belt. Just the sight of him made Cooper shiver.

"Where have ye been, Tuffy?" Blackbeard asked as he bent down on one knee.

Tuffy immediately stood at attention with her tail held high and chest fur puffed out to show respect. Cooper assumed Blackbeard was planning to stroke Tuffy's fur. To Cooper's surprise, the bearded captain reached out to grab him instead. Startled, Cooper took a step back just as JJ Brooks appeared.

"Looks like Cooper doesn't want to go yet," JJ commented.

"He better change his mind. The *Queen* can't hold on much longer," Blackbeard said.

JJ leaned over to grab Como, but the little spider monkey was too clever. Como ran around JJ three times, causing the young pirate to spin in circles as he attempted to catch him.

"Come back here, sneaky monkey!" JJ exclaimed as Como ducked between JJ's legs.

"Remember what I told you," Tuffy warned. "It's better to go peacefully than to put up a fight."

Hearing Tuffy's meows, Blackbeard chuckled. "Sounds like Tuffy has a few things to say about the matter."

"Aye, she's smart. She knows something's wrong with the ship," JJ agreed as he finally managed to capture Como's long, furry tail.

The little spider monkey screeched in protest, but he didn't fight back, allowing JJ to put him into a wooden cage. Meanwhile, Cooper gave in to Blackbeard. Cooper didn't even unsheathe his claws as Blackbeard picked him up and put him in the cage with Como. Surprisingly, the tall, bearded captain put Tuffy in a separate cage.

"Why did Captain put you in your own cage, Tuffy?" Como asked.

"I'm sure he has a good reason," she replied as JJ and Blackbeard tied ropes to the tops of their cages.

Cooper watched the two pirates loop the twisted hemp fiber through the wooden bars of the cage and pull the rope tight to form a knot. They then tossed the opposite end of the rope over a pulley system. Once the ropes were secure, Blackbeard called over a few members of the crew to help them hoist the cages into the air.

With four pirates tugging on the rope together, they easily lifted the cage Cooper and Como were in and maneuvered it over the side of the leaning ship. The cage swung back and forth, causing Cooper to feel a bit sick. It didn't help things when a couple of pirates watching nearby suggested their crewmates get back at Stede Bonnet by dropping Cooper and Como into the water.

Blackbeard threatened to punish the men if they did such, but his words didn't calm Como. The poor little monkey grabbed Cooper and hugged him so tightly Cooper could barely breathe.

"Como, please let go, or at least loosen your grip," Cooper said.

"What if those pirates drop us, and we become shark bait?"

"We need to be brave," Cooper replied.

"Brave?" Como asked in surprise. "When did you become brave?"

"Pirates are brave, Como. I am a pirate cat and you are a pirate monkey. We can do this."

Como relaxed a little as the pirates slowly released the rope, allowing the cage to go down to the waiting periauger. John Martin and JJ's father, Joseph, guided the cage into the small boat and untied the rope. They then hollered at their comrades to send the next cage. Just like before, the pirates slowly lowered Tuffy's cage over the side of the *Queen*. In no time, Tuffy was safely in the periauger beside Cooper and Como. While John secured the cages, Joseph held the rope ladder for JJ. Soon, the young pirate had scurried down the rope ladder and was ready to start rowing when a voice shouted to them from above. Looking up, Cooper spotted Captain Blackbeard leaning over the railing of the *Queen Anne's Revenge.*

Blackbeard gave the pirates a few instructions, but Cooper wasn't listening. Instead, Cooper stared into the captain's bearded face. He studied his wild, black beard and lively, dark eyes. There was something different about him. It was almost as if he were excited. But why? What was causing this sudden change in Blackbeard's attitude? Cooper wasn't sure, but he had a feeling they would soon find out.

Picking up the oars, the three pirates began to row away from the *Queen Anne's Revenge*. Cooper kept his green eyes on the grand ship. The further out they got, the sadder the scene was. From out here, the damage was obvious and painful to look at. *Queen Anne's Revenge* tilted so far to the left, it was as if she was barely holding on and would give in to the waves at any moment.

Surprisingly, it didn't take much effort for the pirates to row the periauger through the inlet. The ocean's waves helped push the boat along until they reached the sound side of the island and had to row the boat ashore. Once they were close to land, several pirates waded into the bright, greenish-blue water to meet them. With the assistance of JJ, Joseph, and John, they were able to pass Cooper and Como's cage to other pirates so they could carry them to dry land.

Since the water was nearly waist high to the men, the bottom of the cage dragged in the water just enough to keep Cooper's paws wet. This only made Como more panicky than he already was. The little monkey's screeches soon became a topic between the pirates as they waded ashore and carried the animals across the sand to the waiting piles of cargo stacked high on the beach.

"Look! It's Cooper and Como," said a familiar voice as the pirates set the cage down and walked away.

Cooper smiled as he recognized Gunner's gray fur through the bars of a wooden cage. Blaze sat beside him in another cage acting frustrated while Prissy purred in excitement from her own. The pirates had also left Marco and Marisol with the three ship's cats. Henrietta, Rooney, and the rest of the chickens were nowhere in sight.

"We are glad to see both of you!" Marisol exclaimed as she ruffled her beautiful scarlet feathers against the wooden bars.

"Yes, we are," Prissy added.

Marco shook his blue tail feathers. "Where's Tuffy?"

"She's right behind us. Captain Blackbeard put her in a separate cage," Cooper explained.

"Are you sure? I don't see her," Blaze said.

"Of course, we're sure. Captain loaded us up at the same time," Como replied. "Those pirates are bringing her over now."

Turning around in the cage, Cooper expected to see his mentor and friend headed their way, but instead discovered an empty beach. The pirates who brought them ashore were now doing something else while JJ, Joseph, and John Martin rowed the periauger toward the *Adventure II* anchored a short distance from land. Tuffy's cage was still in the center of the small boat.

"What are those crazy pirates doing? Why did they take Tuffy with them?" Como asked.

"It appears they are taking her to your ship, Blaze," Gunner said.

"Those chickens were taken over there as well," Marco revealed. "They were on the boat ahead of us. Marisol and I heard poor Henrietta and Rooney clucking the whole way."

"It just doesn't make any sense. Blackbeard ordered everyone to leave the ship, including me," Blaze said.

"Guess I will never see my treasure again," Marisol sighed. "I just hope JJ enjoys my flute as much as that little boy Will did."

The animals continued talking about the flute and the pirates while Cooper watched the scene at the *Adventure II*. By now, JJ, Joseph, and John had reached the ship and were carefully hauling up Tuffy's cage. Moments later, the other two periaugers from the fleet of ships crossed over from the sinking *Queen Anne's Revenge*. Cooper noticed the boats carried only men. Apparently, he wasn't the only one who found this odd. The new activity captured the attention of several pirates on the beach. They alerted their fellow crewmates who quickly located a spyglass.

"What in the blazes!" the pirate holding the spyglass shouted.

"Is something wrong, David?" another pirate asked him.

"Blackbeard and his crew of thieves marooned us on this island."

"Marooned us? What do ye mean?" a third pirate asked as the group of fifty or so pirates gathered around.

"See for yeself," David said as he passed the spyglass to his friend.

"I can't believe it! Those scoundrels are boarding the *Adventure II* and preparing to leave us behind. After all we did, and this is how Blackbeard thanks us. We've got to do something."

"Our hands are tied," David replied. "Blackbeard ordered us to take all the weapons to either the *Adventure II* or the *Revenge*."

"Let's go get them."

"How? Stede Bonnet has one of the periaugers and Blackbeard has the other three. We'll have to wait until Stede returns from Bath."

"Blackbeard is a low-down fox! How could we be so foolish? No wonder William Howard sent so many to the mainland. There's over two hundred men at Fish Town who have no idea what's going on."

"Blackbeard took about a hundred men with him," another pirate pointed out.

"What do ye think Blackbeard plans to do next?"

"I don't know," David replied, "but he never does anything without a reason. He's cunning. Whatever Blackbeard wants, he gets."

Stunned by all this news, Cooper stared at the *Adventure II* as her crew of pirates hauled up the anchor and opened her sails. Even from this distance, Cooper spotted Tuffy's solid black coat standing at her usual post at the bow of the ship. The one-eyed she-cat stood tall with her tail held high and attention turned not toward the inlet, but to the island where she could no doubt see them, too.

Cooper wondered what Tuffy was thinking. Was she sad to see them stranded on this island? Did she have some idea of her own fate? After all, she was a seasoned ship's cat. Perhaps she knew Blackbeard was up to something like this, but chose not to say anything. Regardless of how Tuffy felt, every ship needed a ship's cat and obviously Blackbeard was expecting her to continue her duties.

Someone approached Tuffy from behind. His bushy, black beard was an immediate giveaway. Tuffy and Captain Blackbeard faced the wind as the *Adventure II* turned to pass through the inlet. Blackbeard lifted his three-cornered hat as a sort of salute to those left marooned. He then faced his flagship, the grand *Queen Anne's Revenge* as she lay on her portside, slowly sinking to her watery grave. The tall, bearded captain bowed slightly, as if showing his beloved ship respect.

In an instant, the wind caught the sails, causing them to burst open.

Unlike the massive *Queen*, the *Adventure II* was a smaller and faster ship. Even with her decks packed beyond usual capacity with both cargo and men, she took off with amazing speed toward the north.

Feeling a mixture of sadness and uncertainty, Cooper looked at his friends. What were they going to do now? They were a group of misfit animals with nowhere to go. As Cooper let his green eyes drift to the gathered pirates, he thought about their fate as well. Three hundred pirates couldn't sail away on one ship. None of them could even reach the *Revenge* since Blackbeard's quartermaster, William Howard, had anchored it in the middle of the inlet where the water was the deepest. Like the pirates said, they would have to wait for Stede Bonnet and his small crew to return, assuming Stede had the courage to come back at all.

Suddenly, Cooper had a thought. Instead of seeing this marooning as a bad thing, he started seeing it as a taste of freedom. They were no longer stuck on a ship. Como had figured out a way to unlock the cages when they were at Nassau. He could do it again. This was their chance to truly be free. With the Mighty Creator's help, they could do anything.

A smile crept across Cooper's whiskers as he thought about the possibilities. He quickly got the attention of his friends. If Blackbeard had a plan, then they needed one, too. After all, Cooper was no ordinary cat. He was a pirate cat, and pirates always had a plan in mind, especially when they were planning an adventure.

A Pirate's Life

- Blackbeard went by many names, including Edward Teach and Edward Thatch, but most historians now think his name was Edward Beard.
- We don't know much about Blackbeard before he became a pirate. His birth date, family, and life are all secrets. Many claim he came from Jamaica, Scotland, England, and everywhere in between, but there is no proof of exactly who he was and where he came from.
- Blackbeard was a pirate for roughly two years. Historians believe prior to piracy he was a privateer, legally plundering enemy ships during Queen Anne's War.
- Many men served under Blackbeard during his short career. At one point, there were as many as seven hundred men. When he died, there were only seventeen. The crew members in this book were based on the real pirates.
- The gentleman pirate Stede Bonnet sailed with Blackbeard for many months. Although we don't know if Stede collected exotic

animals, he did keep a large collection of books on his ship. According to records, those who met Stede claimed he acted strange and doubted his ability to be a true pirate captain.

- Blackbeard's prize ship was the *Queen Anne's Revenge*. It was huge compared to most other ships. With *Queen Anne's Revenge* leading the way, Blackbeard and his crew were able to capture many ships as they sailed the Caribbean.

- Pirates often stopped at Nassau to get freshwater, food, and to see their pirate friends. Blackbeard stopped by the island many times during his career. Nassau was a pirate's paradise.

- In May 1718, Blackbeard blockaded what is now Charleston, South Carolina. Although he had the entire port at his mercy, the only thing he requested was a chest of medicine. Many historians believe Blackbeard was sick. The discovery in recent years of a medical instrument found at the wreckage of *Queen Anne's Revenge* supports this claim.

- Blackbeard's ship, *Queen Anne's Revenge*, wrecked off the North Carolina coast near present-day Beaufort in June 1718. Some say it was accidental, but it may have been on purpose to downsize the crew. After abandoning *Queen Anne's Revenge*, Blackbeard transferred supplies, cannons, and men to a smaller ship that he later renamed *Adventure*. He sailed on this ship until his death.

- On Saturday, November 22, 1718, two Royal Navy ships called the *Jane* and the *Ranger* cornered Blackbeard at Ocracoke, North Carolina. Lieutenant Robert Maynard led the attack by water while his comrade, Captain Ellis Brand, came to Bath, North

Carolina, in search of the pirates. The remaining captured pirates of the *Adventure* were all taken to Virginia for trial.

- Lieutenant Maynard discovered Blackbeard's logbook after his death. No one knows what happened to the logbook, but the Colonial and State Records of North Carolina do mention it among Blackbeard's things.

- For over three centuries, treasure hunters have searched North Carolina, other coastal areas on the East Coast, and every island in the Caribbean, but still haven't found Blackbeard's so-called buried treasures.

- We imagine pirate treasure as a chest overflowing with gold, silver, and jewels. Records show pirates did take small amounts of gold or jewels, but it wasn't the main prize. Many stolen "treasures" were cargos of sugar, cocoa, cotton, indigo, and other highly desired merchandise that was scarce in the colonies. Pirates sold the cargo or traded them for supplies. They also stole navigational tools, maps, anchors, sails, weapons, tar for careening, barrels of rum and wine, and anything else they could use.

- Carpenters, coopers, sail makers, and musicians who were on captured ships were either forced into serving or chose to join the pirates. Even doctors were pressed into the ranks.

- Blackbeard is a legendary pirate. Other pirates did kill people as documented in the records. People expect Blackbeard to be an evil man who tortured and killed his victims. Interestingly, there are no records of his supposed murders. He did threaten captives, so it's possible some of his victims may have later died from their injuries. We know more about Blackbeard because of the eyewitness accounts from his victims.

- Cats have served as mousers on ships for hundreds of years. Just like the merchant ships they plundered, pirates needed a ship's cat to take care of the mouse and rat population.

- Like other people, pirates were sometimes superstitious. Legend has it, many sailors and pirates believed having a black cat or at least one with dark-colored fur brought good luck to the ship. Throwing a cat overboard would surely bring bad luck. Oddly, people today think black cats bring bad luck although they don't get as many diseases and therefore typically live longer.

- Unlike human fingernails, a cat's claw connects to the last bone on the toes. A muscle makes the claw unsheathe or come out. To "sheathe" means to cover a sword or knife with a protective case. "Sheathe" also describes the way cat claws retract.

- A cat's sense of smell and touch is sharp. Their eyebrows, whiskers, cheek fur, and ear hair are sensitive to vibrations. Even their nose tip, toes, and paws are sensitive. Their ears have about thirty muscles (humans have six). This gives them the ability to turn their ears in different directions and makes them skilled hunters.

Hope you enjoyed this adventure in history!

Robin Reams

Made in the USA
Middletown, DE
22 March 2023

26750620R00135